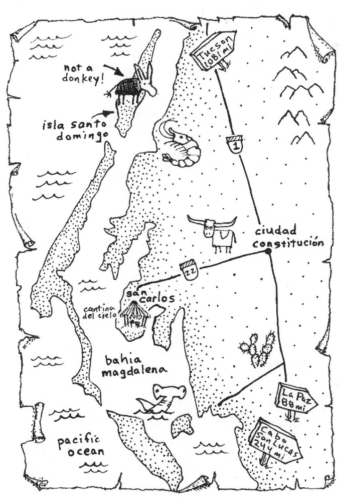

Fish's map of the habitable universe

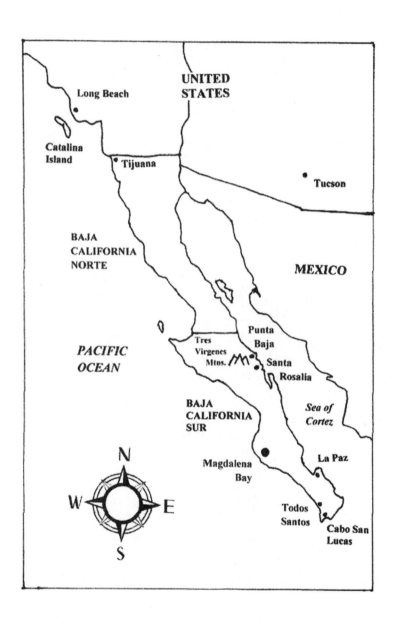

EL DORADO BLUES

EL DORADO BLUES

SHAUN MOREY

THOMAS & MERCER

Text copyright © 2012 Shaun Morey

All rights reserved.

Printed in the United States of America.

Published by Thomas & Mercer

P.O. Box 400818

Las Vegas, NV 89140

ISBN-13: 9781612184982

ISBN-10: 1612184987

For Amanda

According to legend, the word went out that a new, hidden mission was to be constructed in an inaccessible place, and this was to be the storehouse of all the treasure that had been collected by the Jesuits. And, again, according to rumor, this mission was constructed and known as the Mission of Santa Ysabel. The location was kept secret, but it housed all of the wealth which had been accumulated by the Jesuit fathers.

—ERLE STANLEY GARDNER, *HOVERING OVER BAJA*

CHAPTER ONE

Tres Virgenes, Baja California Sur

Digby hardly noticed the heat. Or the squall of rock exploding around him. He lowered the pickax to the ground and raised the bottle of tequila. Herradura Añejo. His first swig since leaving Tucson less than twenty-four hours earlier, stuffing two pairs of jeans, a handful of T-shirts, and a well-worn dopp kit into a duffel bag. The twelve-foot aluminum skiff secured to the rack above the bed of his F-150 pickup truck was a prop this time. As was the 15-horsepower Yamaha outboard bungeed to the sidewall, fishing gear tossed in like flotsam.

Not that Digby didn't fish. He did. As a tenured archaeologist at the University of Arizona, Professor Duncan Rigby fished often. Mostly, it was along Baja's remote coastline, to fill the gaps while hunting for lost missions and the legendary Jesuit Treasure. He'd written his dissertation on the Jesuits, had written books about their exploits across Mexico. But this was no scholarly trip. Nor was it another excuse to go fishing. The angling implements were simply cover for the sharpened pickax buried deep inside his sleeping bag. A ruse to hide the ring of skeleton keys, the miniature butane torch, and the ancient parchment map stuffed inside his fanny pack and wedged between bottles of booze.

Serious booze.

Yucca gold.

Tequila.

After twenty years teaching archaeology to insipid collegiates, battling inept department heads, and watching his salary erode like sandstone, Digby deserved a good buzz. And a bit of luck.

Now, as he took a break from digging, he rubbed his red-rilled eyes and toasted to that good luck. He took a long pull from the bottle and savored its burn, the tawny liquid coursing down his throat like an electric eel. He wiped the wetness from his blond mustache and glanced at his right arm, coated with dust. The fine powder turned muddy with sweat, blurring the image of the life-size megalodon shark tooth tattooed across his forearm.

The tattoo was an exact replica of Digby's most sensational find. Fossilized shark's teeth were not uncommon in Baja's high desert, but the discovery of what was thought to be the world's largest and most powerful predators sent waves of excitement through the archaeology department back in Tucson. Digby had once again been searching for the famed Jesuit Treasure—Baja's version of El Dorado—when he unearthed the enormous incisor.

The perfectly preserved shark tooth measured more than seven inches in length and nearly three inches in width. It was one of the largest ever found. Digby knew the tooth was more of an academic gold mine than a monetary one, so he donated it to the campus museum where it went on display with his photograph and a brief biography. That had been three years ago. Three long years without an archaeological encore.

Until now.

Digby set the tequila in his knapsack and breathed in the heat of the desert. Dust mostly, and the incenselike odor of a lone elephant tree. Digby wiped grit from his brow and glanced around the canyon.

It was no wonder civilization bypassed Baja California. The mountains of the eastern Vizcaino were as arid as the desert hardpan below. Heat radiated from the cliffs like steam from a flatiron, and other than the blossoming elephant tree and a lone Palo Adan tree hanging from a cleft fifty feet above, its thorny arms splayed outward like a witch's broom, nothing but creosote bushes sprouted between the boulders. Everything else was rock and sand. No birds chirped and no breeze descended down the narrow ravine. But for the occasional buzz of an insect, the afternoon was dead calm.

And sweltering.

Digby ignored the temperature. Thirty years tracking antiquity across the desert had given him a lizard's immunity to triple-digit heat. The tequila helped. Thoughts of treasure helped more. Digby grasped the pick, his mind racing over centuries of myth and lore. Millions in Jesuit gold and silver and pearls rumored to be hidden in Baja California. Hastily concealed before the Jesuits were expelled by the king of Spain. Most historians thought the tale nonsense.

Digby knew otherwise. He also knew the cache was close.

Very close.

The signs were unmistakable. Hard-packed sand had become homogeneous rock. First the layer of small pebbles, and then the blankets of fist-size rocks. All of it packed tightly by the vicissitudes of time. Countless flash floods careening through the canyon matting down the terrain. Tons of water tightening the gaps between the rubble, filtering alluvium from slag. Digby recognized the oddity of so many similarly sized rocks set geometrically beneath the sand.

Decades of excavation had taught him that Mother Nature was messy with her burials.

Man was methodical.

Digby stepped into the gravelike depression and considered his good fortune. Just twenty-four hours earlier, he'd been planning a summer course syllabus on the lost missions of Baja California. Huddled in the basement of the campus museum, he'd come across a trunk of ancient Jesuit journals. Standard diaries he'd seen a hundred times before: ramblings of old priests complaining about depraved Indians, despicable living conditions, and Baja's uninhabitable wasteland.

A depressing read had it not been for the stainless-steel flask Digby had smuggled into the museum. Tipsy and bored, he'd handled the old trunk carelessly, and the bottom fell out. Literally. A false floor had slipped from its groove, revealing a sheaf of old parchment wrapped in oilskin. Parchment that held a crudely drawn map of Baja California with directions written in Spanish. The destination was a mountain range known as Tres Virgenes.

Three virgins.

The headline on the map read: *PROPRIEDAD DEL DIOS* PROPERTY OF GOD

Digby quickly repacked the trunk, tucked the oilskin and its parchment into the waistband of his pants, and hurried back to his office at the university's archaeology department. He notified the head of the department of a sudden family emergency, e-mailed his travel plans to his sister, and headed south.

Deep into Baja's Vizcaino Desert. Digby knew the landscape well. He'd crossed it many times in his search for missions.

He drove through the night avoiding gun-toting *federales*, inebriated big-rig drivers, cattle-size potholes, and death-crazed cyclists intent on pedaling the shoulderless two-lane road known as Mexico's Highway 1. He reached Tres Virgenes at dawn, and spent the next six hours traversing a web of spine-jarring dirt roads furrowed by washboards the size of camel humps.

Mercifully, his south-of-the-border junket ended when all four tires of his pickup sank axle-deep into the soft sands of an arroyo bordered by the sheerest cliffs Digby had ever encountered.

He grabbed his fanny pack, the pickax, a gallon of water, and a bottle of Añejo. Three hours later he arrived at a rock face marred by massive veins of quartz. The white mineral coursed upward and was intersected by an equally enormous horizontal fissure. The effect was as surreal as it was supernatural: a nearly perfect replica of a life-size cross.

Digby dropped his gear and toasted to the heavens. Then he paced off the requisite steps written on the map and began to dig.

Now, half an hour later, adrenaline thrust him into overdrive. Storms of shale and spall burst from the ground. Ropes of sweat braided his skin. He swung again and again. The heavy pick shattered earth. Digby was in a rhythm, a digging trance, that rare state of archaeological bliss hovering at the edge of great discoveries. A state of semiconsciousness reserved for dinosaur hunters, tomb raiders, and pyramid dwellers. Legend seekers.

Treasure hunters.

Digby felt the skin on his arms tingle with each blow. Rumors of the Jesuit Treasure had persisted for hundreds of years, but no proof had ever surfaced. Old missions had been scoured steeple to pulpit, some even dismantled and left to ruin. Most hunters were amateur sleuths who relinquished their dreams of riches after underestimating the desert heat. Others spent their lives prospecting the arid surroundings only to conclude that no treasure existed. And a few desert lovers, like the author Erle Stanley Gardner, spent a fortune in vain, content with the discovery of caves graffitied in ancient hieroglyphics.

Digby swung the ax again, and heard the unmistakable thud of solid wood. He dropped to his knees and clawed at the loosened rock. He paused to wipe his eyes—eyes mapped with exhaustion, eyes glazed with tequila. Something moved in his peripheral vision and he jerked back with a start. A tarantula had tired of the commotion and was ambling into a crevice of shade.

He settled himself with another swig of tequila, then returned to excavating. Moments later he brushed dust from the rough-hewn top of the creosote-treated trunk. He ran a callused hand over the lid and mouthed the words burned into the wood in large lettering, weathered but still legible:

PROPRIEDAD DEL DIOS

PROPERTY OF GOD

Thrill clouded Digby's vision. A loud turbulence filled his head. Despite the abundance of tequila his mouth felt dry. He steadied himself with a series of deep breaths, hoisted the pick, and carefully worked from his knees to expand a wide moat around the trunk.

A heavy padlock came into view, its ornate faceplate corroded, its keyhole preserved with beeswax. He reached into his fanny pack and removed a ring of variously sized skeleton keys borrowed from the artifacts room of the campus museum. Digby worked through the set of keys, ignoring his trembling hands.

Ten minutes later the lock remained unopened. He returned the keys to his pack and freed a pocket-size butane blowtorch and a ball-peen hammer. He heated the shackle, and after a few persuasive strikes watched the lock fall open and drop to the rocks.

Digby grasped the front of the heavy lid and gently tugged upward. The hinges complained loudly as the desert air rushed in, and for the first time in more than three hundred years, the inside of the trunk glittered with sunlight.

He heard himself gasp in the stilted air.

Hundreds of pearls spilled like hailstones across the treasure. Piles of solid gold pesos accompanied bejeweled rings. There were silver ingots and crosses inlaid with rubies and diamonds. Rosaries gleamed celestially. Golden crucifixes sparkled. Silver-coated clamshells held mounds of opulent jewelry. There were solid silver idols, ornately carved pendants, and golden charms of every size.

Digby carefully removed the top layer of treasure and spotted the silver spikes of the famed and priceless centerpiece: a crown of thorns carved from a sacred whale bone, dipped into liquid silver, and then blanketed with black pearls. A gift from the local Indians who'd been converted by the priests.

Those who believed in the treasure said the crown was cursed. Others thought it all nonsense. Digby hefted it with care, and then gently placed it back into the trunk.

He slapped his blue-jeaned thigh and guffawed like a madman. He danced in a circle and whooped with glee. The legends were true! The Jesuits *had* accumulated a trove of wealth only to bury it before their exile!

Before the greedy monarch could confiscate it.

Before the indigenous Indians could destroy it.

Before the revolutionaries could steal it.

Digby wasn't a religious man, but he felt himself lean back and look to the heavens. He knew it would take more than luck to get the precious cargo home where he could catalog each piece safely. Maybe cull a few pieces for a black-market retirement before reporting the find to the Mexican consulate. Buy a fishing boat and retire down south. Let his fame evolve over time. Spend his days chasing billfish while his reputation soared. Wait for his name to one day emboss that legendary scroll of diggers: the Leakeys, Sir Arthur Evans, or maybe Hollywood's next Indiana Jones.

Digby dropped his head and closed his eyes.

Had he kept them open, he might have spied the two scraggly men entering the canyon with bloodshot eyes and crooked smiles.

Expatriated Americans with loot on their minds.

Ex-felons holding guns.

Treasure hunters.

CHAPTER TWO

Magdalena Bay, Baja California Sur

Atticus Fish shut the leather-backed accounting book and stood from the desk at the back of his bar, Cantina del Cielo. He changed into a fresh pair of sailcloth pants and a loose-fitting safari-style shirt. He recinched the machete to his thigh, and strolled barefoot across the sand-packed floor past handcrafted driftwood tables toward the circular bar. It was nearly sunset, and the happy hour crowd had left their seats to school like sardines at the front of the open-air cantina. Fish poured himself a soda. High above, in the rafters of Baja's largest *palapa*, a scarlet macaw named Chuy squawked with excitement.

"What's the word, Sandman?" asked a tall, dark-skinned Indian. The man stood inside the horseshoe-shaped bar made from the deck of a shipwrecked schooner. The old wood was preserved with a new coat of varnish and sat atop an apron of cactus ribs.

"You bartending for me now?" Fish asked, his thumb and forefinger twirling the crimp at the end of his braided goatee.

"Naw, man, I only make the hooch," he said and poured a Tecate into an icy mug. "Isabela's out front. Time for the green flash special. What do you think?"

"Fifty-fifty."

"Ah, hell. You always say that," Skegs complained. He leaned over and scratched the belly of a drunken iguana lying on its side in a puddle of spilled beer. The iguana rolled to its feet and wobbled toward a second lizard passed out at the far bend of the bar.

"Sixty-forty?" Fish hedged.

"The house or the customers?"

"Both."

Fish glanced through the open windows, taking in the panoramic view of Magdalena Bay. He scanned the smattering of sailboats anchored in the shallows, and then paused at his fifty-six-foot trawler, *Fish Goddess*. Unlike most trawlers south of the border, this one glimmered in a rust-free skin of emerald green paint. At the helm was state-of-the-art navigational equipment connected to a pair of turbo Caterpillar engines and a brushed aluminum hull that could cut through rough seas like a finback whale.

But what interested Fish most was the attack vessel hidden on the back deck. A personalized submarine with twin titanium blades capable of snipping piano wire like floss. Fish felt his heart skip a beat at the thought.

No larger than a picnic table, the one-man sub had arrived two nights earlier under a moonless sky. Covertly delivered to Fish by ocean freighter a mile outside the bay, it was quickly transferred to the refurbished trawler. An all-cash transaction with a hefty bonus for the Canadian captain and crew to forget all about the delivery. The fewer people who knew of the underwater weapon the better.

"Sun's about to set," Skegs said, snapping Fish from his reverie.

Fish followed Skegs to the front entrance and stopped beside a group of sunburned surfers and dusty off-roaders. They stared at the watery horizon waiting for the sun to drift into the sea. A light breeze ruffled the *palapa* fronds above their heads and brought the scent of mud and iodine from the exposed roots of the nearby mangroves. Isabela, the cantina's bartender, aimed a digital camera and counted down the seconds in Spanish.

"*Diez, nueve, ocho!*" she called out to the whoops of the crowd.

Fish and Skegs averted their eyes, and as the sun swooned into the sea, they saw the flicker of green hover over the horizon like frog breath. The bar exploded in celebration.

Isabela held out the camera and announced to the happy crowd, "Green flash *especial.* Next cerveza's *en la casa!*"

The patrons rushed back inside. Isabela winked at Fish, and then followed the crowd to her station behind the bar.

"You ready?" Fish asked Baja's premier bootlegger.

"Does a wahoo piss in the sea?"

Fish wrinkled his brow.

"Pretty good, huh?"

"Stick to selling mescal."

An hour later and less than a mile from shore, Skegs slowed the trawler. Bobbing on the horizon were the bright lights of an unlicensed commercial long-liner, its decks glowing like a bonfire. Skegs purposely kept the trawler's running lights off, and eased to within a quarter-mile of the illegal vessel. Fish, meanwhile, removed the tarp and attached the hydraulic lift to the custom-made sub, careful not to damage the hinged robotic arm with its twin titanium rotors.

The wealthy expatriate opened the hatch and folded his six-foot-four-inch frame inside. He powered up the instrument panel, checking the fuel level in the closed-cycle diesel system responsible for charging the battery-powered craft. Satisfied, he poked his head from the cockpit and gave Skegs a thumbs-up. The mescal maker hurried down from the helm.

"Give 'em hell, Davy Jones," Skegs said and closed the watertight hatch. He manipulated the hydraulic lift and raised the submarine from its chocks. A swell rolled beneath the trawler, and he gently lowered the sub into the sea.

Skegs waited for the submarine to sink from sight. Then he hurried inside and retrieved his six-foot Shimano Tallus big-game fishing rod fitted with a gold Tiagra reel. He rigged a dead squid soaked in tuna oil to a size-nine circle hook crimped to the end of fifteen feet of wire leader. He attached a breakaway cement weight and a green Cyalume glow stick to the swivel.

"Bombs away!" he called out happily, while dropping the swordfish bait over the side.

CHAPTER THREE

Tres Virgenes, Baja California Sur

"Well, well," the kidnapper said. He pointed a semiautomatic Ruger at Digby's chest. "Look what we've got here."

His twin brother aimed an identical gun and nodded. "Looks like professor-boy found something."

"Something shiny and gold."

The brother bobbed his head up and down, nearly losing his Angels baseball cap. "You tell him, Zack."

"This is government property," Digby stated, his tequila buzz quickly retreating.

"Government property?" Zack scoffed. He wore a Dodgers cap low to his brow. "Does he look Mexican to you, Jack?"

Jack slapped his thigh and spit a stream of tobacco juice onto the rocks. "Maybe an albino Mexican."

The twins laughed, their long, dishwater beards waving beneath their chins.

Digby waited for the laughter to stop and said, "I'm an archaeologist hired by the Mexican government to search for historical artifacts."

"You mean buried treasure," Zack said.

"Jesuit priests collected these artifacts," Digby continued. "On behalf of the church. The Mexican government is the rightful owner."

"Rightful owner? The guys who buried it are long dead. I figure if they wanted the church or the government to have it, they wouldn't have hid it way out here in the boondocks."

"Hallelujah," Jack agreed and sent another missile of dark juice into the dirt.

Digby shook his head. "We're on Mexican land. That means the Mexican people are entitled to these artifacts."

"Why's he keep calling it that, Zack?" Jack asked.

"He thinks we're stupid." Zack waved the gun at Digby. "You think we're stupid, don't you?"

"I never said that."

"But you were thinking it."

"I was thinking you two have guns and I'm all alone out here."

"You've got us to keep you company."

"Uh-huh," Jack agreed.

"Kind of like bodyguards," Zack said, his eyes flittering to the cliff face, where the tarantula was moving from its crevice.

"Always wanted to be a bodyguard," Jack said.

Zack glared at Digby. "Those *artifacts*, as you call it, are going back with us."

"Um, Zack?"

Zack turned an annoyed glance at Jack.

"Wasn't we just supposed to follow and see what he did with the loot?"

"That was before."

"Before what?"

"Before we saw how much there was."

"You sure Mr.—?"

"Shut up, Jack!"

"Someone sent you to follow me?" Digby asked.

Zack's lips unveiled a mouthful of crooked teeth. "No, we just happened to be hiking around in this godforsaken shithole sweating our asses off and getting sunburned because we got nothing better to do."

Jack took aim and drenched the tarantula with a cheekful of brown spittle. The spider fell from the cliff and slogged its way toward the safety of a nearby boulder. "I thought you was supposed to be smart," he said, removing his Angels cap and wiping the sweat from his brow.

Digby sighed.

Zack said, "Listen up, Jack. As for us taking custody of the treasure, it shows initiative."

Jack dropped his head. "Sorry, Zack."

Digby cleared his throat. "Where do you plan to take it?"

"Tie him up, Jack."

Jack removed a length of rope from his back pocket and motioned for Digby to hold out his hands. "Don't make me shoot you, Professor."

As Jack cinched the rope, Digby asked, "How'd you find me?"

"A blind man could have tracked you across the border."

"You followed me all the way from Tucson?"

Jack glanced nervously at Zack. "I never said nothing about Tucson." He spit with a defiant shrug of his shoulders.

"Only one person knows I'm down here. Who—"

"Save your breath," Zack interrupted. "We've got a long walk back to the trucks. All night, by the looks of that trunk."

"Then what?"

"Then we decide whether to keep you alive or feed you to the scorpions."

CHAPTER FOUR

Ten Miles off Magdalena Bay, Baja California Sur

Atticus Fish reclined the pilot seat of his minisubmarine and closed his eyes. The currents were light ten miles off Magdalena Bay, and the autopilot was locked onto the path of the illegal long-liner. The whirring blades above his head caused an occasional vibration in the cockpit, but Fish hardly noticed. Lyle Lovett crooned through the helm speakers about riding a horse on a boat, and Fish wondered how his mule, Mephistopheles, would do out on the sea.

"You out there, Subman?" came the sudden sound of Skegs's voice over the VLF radio.

Fish opened his eyes.

"Hey, man, you coming up for air soon?"

Fish turned down the music and unhinged the microphone. He glanced at the sonar screen and said, "These pricks set hooks halfway to Cabo."

"That's a lot of turtle soup."

"Not anymore."

Fish was pleased with the progress of his inaugural underwater mission. For months he had grown increasingly incensed by the influx of illicit long-liners working closer and closer to the coastline. Long-liner captains claiming to target nonexistent sharks, but using loopholes in the law to haul millions of pounds of game fish and turtles from the water. Setting miles of hooks where sharks no longer roamed. Boating tons of juvenile dorado, tuna, and marlin that the government considered bycatch under its lax sharking regulations. Miles of indiscriminate death traps floating beneath the surface capable of snaring anything and everything. Dolphins, whales, and manta rays were often caught and quickly rendered as bait or released with hooks imbedded in their throats. Millions of creatures left maimed and dying each year. And all of it ignored by a corrupt fisheries department skimming kickbacks by the boatload.

Atticus Fish may have been a foreigner, but as a wealthy ex-attorney who'd sued the Almighty and won, he knew how to win a nefarious war.

Subterfuge.

Now, with the submarine locked on course, its twin blades slicing monofilament every hundred feet, Fish felt the rush of vindication.

"Tell me again how much you spent on that thing?" Skegs asked.

"Two million. Plus another million for the blades. Diamond infused and laser sharpened."

"Million bucks for a blade? Hell, I could have rigged something for half that price. Probably made it deadlier, too. Buffalo-knife sharp."

"You skinned buffaloes?"

"Aw, man, why are you always insulting my race? My forefathers lived off of the land. Buffalo meat was their subsistence. They passed the knowledge down to the young ones."

"I've seen you skin a fish. It's not pretty."

"I'm going to skin a rich gringo if you keep it up."

"How's the weather up top?"

"Light rollers, stars blazing, low seventies, perfect. Except the fishing. Haven't had a sniff all night."

"Hence the reason I'm down here."

"Long-liners done pissed off an Indian now."

"Sit tight, Geronimo. Things will get interesting soon enough."

"Geronimo? Why not Crazy Horse? Or Pancho Villa?"

"I'm signing off now."

"Toozie called."

"She called on the boat phone?" Fish asked, worried.

"Naw, man. She called the bar. Isabela patched her through to me."

"Everything alright?"

"Don't really know. She said something about a *norteamericano* gone missing. Some archaeologist doing research on the lost missions. Sounds to me like he might have found the gold."

"Gold?"

"Jesuit booty. And lots of it. Supposed to be millions hidden out in the desert somewhere."

"When?"

"Hundreds of years ago."

"No, when did he go missing?"

"Few days ago. Missed a school meeting up north."

"And Toozie's heading our way?"

"Not yet. She asked for your help. Said the missing dude was going into the Tres Virgenes. But she didn't know exactly what part. Wondered if you'd do a flyover and look for his truck. I told her you were doing a fly*under* at the moment. A little batfish boogie, but that you'd call back as soon as you surface."

"Batfish boogie?"

"Code for sabotaging the long-liners, man. You and your underwater Batmobile."

"Batmobile?"

"You like it? I was thinking I could paint the sub superhero style. Give it gills and teeth. Call it the Batfish. Maybe add some gnarly graphics. Couple of big moray eels with bloody fangs. What do you think?"

"I think I'm hanging up."

"I'll bang out a couple of mock-ups for you. If you don't like the morays you might like the zombie flying fish."

Fish started to place the microphone on its hook when he heard Skegs mention a familiar name.

"Say again?"

"I said she also mentioned that rich cat, Ronald Stump, agreed to meet you in La Paz tomorrow afternoon."

Fish didn't respond.

"You selling out on me, Sandman?"

"Not a chance."

"Swear on the *Fish Goddess*?"

"You'll be the first to know."

"I really can't paint your sub?"

"Really."

Fish replaced the microphone and turned up the music. Lyle Lovett had finished riding his horse on a boat, and Lowell George was reminiscing about smuggling folks and smokes from Mexico. Fish's broad shoulders jitterbugged to the beat. He was excited at the prospect of working with Toozie again. She was more than an ex-sister-in-law. She was a fearless PI who'd helped him save the crew of the *Wahoo Rhapsody* a year earlier, helped him take down the corrupt federal prosecutor posing as an international drug dealer. She was also single and attractive.

Fish had invited her to his island to celebrate their victory, but she had yet to make it down. Maybe this time would be different. Maybe this time they could work the case from southern Baja. Find the missing archaeologist together. Then maybe he'd show her how to catch Magdalena Bay's elusive black snook. He smiled at the thought.

First things first, though. He had miles of fishing line to cut. Thousands of hooks to destroy.

Batfish boogie, Skegs called it.

Not bad, he had to admit.

CHAPTER FIVE

Long Beach, California

Harvey Dixon stood in the parking lot of the Museum of Latin American Art near downtown Long Beach. In the distance, off-shore oil tankers spat exhaust as they awaited escort into Los Angeles Harbor. It was midafternoon and heat hovered above the asphalt like a toxic phantom. An anemic breeze brought little relief, and the air smelled heavily of burnt petroleum.

Harvey held a cigarette in one hand, a cell phone in the other. Behind him the museum's contemporary building sat like a mono-lith. Towering palms did little to hide the eccentric design. Nor did the bright-blue silo wedged between perpendicular frames of two-story concrete. From a distance, the presentation resembled something out of a psychotropic art class. Up close, it looked like a futuristic water treatment plant. And no matter the perspective, there was utterly nothing Latin about it.

Harvey didn't care what the place looked like as long as it housed expensive art. Which is why he had arranged for the job as security guard. Arranged for the early retirement of the old guard. Followed by the phony references and the counterfeit identification. Child's play for a man of Harvey's talents.

Then, just as he was planning a heist of selected Aztec carv-ings, his plans had changed. His brother Slim was suddenly headed for Baja. Headed down to intercept a load of treasure far greater than anything Harvey could ever hope to plunder state-side. He dialed the cell phone.

"The mother lode's been found," he whispered.

"The mother lode?" came a muffled voice.

"What?" Harvey asked. "Your voice is breaking up."

"I'm in a meeting."

"Huh?"

"What fucking mother lode?" the voice barked.

Harvey puffed at his cigarette. "The whole enchilada. Church artifacts. Buried by dead priests hundreds of years ago."

There was a pause. "The Jesuit Treasure?"

"Glad you're listening."

"How certain are you?"

"Slim left this morning. A couple of brothers stole it from the archaeologist who found it."

"What archaeologist?"

"Who gives a shit? He'll never make it back. Neither will the others."

"Who else knows?"

"The usual cast of characters."

"Bullshit. Who hired Slim?"

"How soon can you and your yacht get to Cabo?"

"You didn't answer my question."

Harvey flicked the butt to the ground and mashed it into the asphalt with the heel of his boot. "Slim says you can have it all for ten million. He'll even load it onto your boat. We want cash, of course. Offshore accounts. You know the drill."

"You tell Slim he's been sniffing the glue too long."

"He said it's worth ten times that amount. More if we piece it out. The Europeans love this kind of shit. Anything Baja and they get a royal boner. You ever hear about that British dude who walked the whole peninsula? Nearly died doing it, so you know what he did? He came back and did it again. By mule. Crazy fuckers, those Brits."

"Tell Slim I'll go five. But I need to see it first. All of it."

"He said you'd say that."

"Before anyone else."

"He won't come unless it's ten."

"He will if he wants to get out of Mexico alive."

Harvey heard the phone disconnect. He freed another cigarette from its pack and lit it with a steady hand. He scrolled through his phone list and stopped at another familiar name. He sent the call and listened to it ring. As it went to message, he inhaled a lungful of smoke and then repeated his offer to sell the treasure. This time the price was twenty million.

Two down, one to go, he said to himself and made a third call.

CHAPTER SIX

Ten Miles off Magdalena Bay, Baja California Sur

Minutes after surfacing from his underwater offensive, Fish stood in the salon of the refurbished trawler, a tall glass of warm *horchata* in one hand, a satellite telephone in the other. His long hair had curled in the humid submarine and it just brushed past his wide shoulders. Skegs sat at the helm steering a course for Magdalena Bay, where the seaplane sat moored in the shallow waters in front of Cantina del Cielo. High above, the early morning stars swept across the sky like glittering currents.

Fish dialed. As he waited for the connection, he watched through the open door as a rising wind caught the corner of the canvas submarine tarp. The tie-down unraveled and began to flap against the side of the glistening vessel. Fish hurried out to the deck, cupping the phone between his chin and shoulder and quickly retied the line. As he turned toward the stern, he spotted a pair of sooty terns flittering across the boat's wake, their compact wings flashing in the starlight.

"McGill Detective Agency," came the familiar female voice.

"Heard you were looking for a man with a mule."

"Really?" she said. "That's the best you could come up with?"

"I actually do own a mule."

"I'm supposed to be impressed?"

"I'm a little short on sleep."

"Skegs mentioned an all-nighter. You back on the bottle?"

"Wrong kind of all-nighter."

"Is there a right kind?"

He explained the recent influx of illegal long-liners, and then said, "Wiped out forty miles of monofilament tonight."

Toozie whistled. "The mule joke's funnier all of a sudden." She paused. "You tracked forty miles worth of hooks without being detected?"

"Submarines are stealthy."

"You can't be serious."

"Custom-made. Delivered to the bay a couple of nights ago. On the sly, of course."

"That must have cost a fortune. How—?" She caught herself, and laughed. "Well done, Atticus. The fish gods must be having a hell of a fiesta tonight."

"First of many, I hope."

Toozie paused. "I need your help."

"The missing archaeologist?"

"He sent an e-mail to his sister before he left. Said he found out where the Jesuits buried their treasure. Somewhere in the Tres Virgenes mountain range. Said if he wasn't back in two days to call me. She called me late last night."

"You know this guy?"

"Not personally. I met the sister at a cocktail party about a year ago. University functions I get invited to. Sometimes I give out business cards."

"So the brother never called her."

"Nope."

Fish crossed the deck and entered the quietude of the salon. "Two days to drive down to the Tres Virgenes, dig up the treasure, and drive back home seems uncomfortably tight. He must have been in a hell of a hurry."

"If it's true—that he found the Jesuit Treasure—it's worth tens of millions of dollars. Maybe more if you're the superstitious type." She hesitated and then said, "Some say it's cursed."

"Cursed?"

"I've been doing research. Apparently, one of the Indians enslaved by the Jesuits presented Padre Kino with a crown. It was carved from a sacred whale bone, dipped in silver, and embedded with black pearls."

"And cursed?"

"Whether or not it's true, some very powerful people would go to great lengths to get it."

"Like Ronald Stump," Fish commented.

"Exactly."

"Skegs mentioned you were able to set up a meeting with the blowhard. I can fly the reconnaissance afterward."

"That would be great. Maybe just check the access roads into the Tres Virgenes. See if you can spot the F-150. The neighbor said Digby left in a hurry with an aluminum skiff on top."

"Happy to look around." Fish stared through the galley window at the approaching lights of San Carlos and the dock in front of his bar. The wind had dropped inside the bay, and the surface spilled inland like an obsidian lake. "How'd you do it, Toozie?"

"Which part?"

"Stump. The meeting. How did you get him to meet with me? In person rather than sending some assistant?"

"You know. The basics. Wit, charm, poise, and grace."

"And humility, clearly."

Toozie laughed. "I might have mentioned your considering the sale of the island. But only if he agreed to meet you in person…due to your personal issues, paranoia, financial difficulties, etcetera."

"You told him I'd sell?"

"The man needed a little motivation. Besides, *considering* a sale doesn't mean selling."

"You lied."

"I like to call it finessing the truth."

It was Fish's turn to laugh. "Come down and work the case from here. Free room and board. Great fishing. Million-dollar view."

"Tempting."

"But?"

"But I need to work a few angles from this end. Maybe *after* we find the archaeologist."

Fish felt a smile creep across his face. "Fair enough. What time am I meeting Stump?"

"Midafternoon. And don't be late. He's got appointments in Cabo San Lucas the next day. Needs to leave La Paz no later than six or so in the evening."

"I won't be late."

"Atticus?"

"Still here."

"Try to be civil with the man."

Fish reached up and twirled the metal crimp at the end of his goatee.

"Where's the fun in that?"

CHAPTER SEVEN

Cabo San Lucas, Baja California Sur

Charlie Diamond reclined in his custom big-game fishing chair on the back of his yacht and eyed a stray dog rooting in a dock-side bin for fish heads. The flickering dock lights illuminated its skintight coat mottled with mange and stretched tightly over its ribcage. Its ears were notched and scarred, and its tail hung crookedly as though hinged in the middle. It paused to sniff the night air, and then resumed its search for scraps.

Charlie snatched a four-ounce pyramid sinker from the drawer beneath his feet and crept to the stern. The dog raised its head a second time, and Charlie heaved the lead weight. It soared over the dock, skipped across the concrete causeway, glanced off the trash bin, and struck the dog's foreleg. The animal yelped and sprang away into the darkness. Charlie raised his chubby arms in celebration. He pirouetted on his canvas Docksiders, skipped happily into the boat's saloon, and mixed himself a Cape Cod.

Charlie wore a white captain's shirt patterned in nautical wheels, dark-blue cotton slacks, and despite the late hour, a pair of Maui Jim polarized sunglasses. A Hemingway fishing cap camouflaged his receding hairline. He lit a Cuban cigar and turned up the volume on the stereo. Foreigner's "Hot Blooded" filled the room, the high decibels jangling the teardrop crystals of the saloon's oversize chandelier. Charlie puffed on the cigar and watched tendrils of smoke swirl into the teakwood slats of the boat's ventilation system. He glanced past the stuffed blue marlin to the quartz wall clock fashioned into a miniature nautical wheel.

Eleven o'clock.

Showtime.

Charlie plucked his money clip and cell phone from the marbled bar. The phone's message light was blinking. Charlie ignored it and strolled back to the deck of the sixty-eight-foot Bertram, eponymously named *King of Diamonds*. His *Ace of Diamonds* awaited him back at Redondo Beach, where he lived and managed his billboard empire aboard the seventy-eight-foot Nordhavn berthed at King Harbor. It was also where he housed most of his black-market loot. Mexican artifacts mostly: Mayan statues, pre-Columbian jade figures, Aztec stone calendars, gold Inca gods and goddesses, and an array of silver jewelry fashioned for the dead.

Some were bought directly from treasure hunters whom Charlie met through antique coin dealers. Others were acquired with the aid of the American businesswoman who owned Cabo's most famous gentlemen's club, the Pink Octopus. A front for laundering her black-market art.

The woman, known only as Barbie, demanded filter masks be worn during meetings, which were always held in her sterilized lair. An extreme mysophobe, Barbie covered her shaved head and eyebrowless face with so much antibacterial lotion that her skin shined like a salamander's hide. She wore clothes infused with silver threads to ward off bacteria, and managed her affairs via state-of-the-art electronics: listening devices, cameras, motion sensors.

The only time she ever left her inner sanctum was during the predawn hours, when the streets of Cabo were empty and the air unstirred by human breath and car exhaust. Even then she wore a filter mask and surgical gloves. Charlie didn't give a shit if the woman wore a hazmat suit. She was well connected with the black-market antiquities dealers, and her all-cash prices were unbeatable.

At the moment, however, Charlie wasn't thinking of Barbie or her illicit loot. He'd flown in that evening after endless stateside meetings with power-hungry bureaucrats: county commissioners who controlled freeway real estate; city councilmen worried about vociferous neighbors; zoning personnel reluctant to raise height restrictions. All of them thieves in need of old-fashioned persuasion: payola. Preferably in the form of untraceable cash. Charlie was happy to oblige. He reveled in the power of graft. The perks of greed. Ethics were for the poor, and Charlie was adamant about staying rich.

He eyed the matching yacht berthed beside him and grinned. The *Queen of Diamonds*, his smallest and most favored boat, lounged triumphantly in her slip, a gold-colored tuna tower embellishing her modest fifty-eight-foot length. A vase of flowers rose prominently from the filet table, where a lush golden carpet led visitors inside to the master stateroom. The maid had turned down the bed earlier that evening, dimming the lights just enough for Charlie's hidden camera to record all the action. Twenty-two scenes and counting. Charlie might have made his millions in billboards, but after spending nearly every other weekend in Cabo this year, he fancied himself more porn star than real estate tycoon.

Charlie strode up the gangway and flung open the gate. Summertime in Cabo San Lucas.

Prime marlin season.

Primo tourist season.

Charlie Diamond hunted them both.

CHAPTER EIGHT

Ensenada, Baja California Sur

Slim Dixon glanced down at the cell phone in his hand. The caller ID read "International." He pressed the earpiece snugly into place and took another sip from the Gran Patron in his shot glass. In the background, a mariachi band played "Guantanamera" to the delight of a sunburned American couple in matching straw hats. The couple shared a basket of shell-roasted peanuts and sucked down matching Bloody Marys. It was nine in the morning and the bar was packed.

"They should have checked in by now," came an angry, American voice through the earpiece.

"Uh-huh," Slim said, distractedly scraping a boot heel through the layer of peanut shells.

"Did you hear me, goddammit?!"

"Yep."

"Turn that fucking music down!"

"Can't do that, boss."

"Why the hell not?"

"Because it's live."

"Live? Where the hell are you?"

"Hussong's."

"What?"

"Hussong's. It's a cantina in Ensenada."

"I know what it is. What the hell are you doing in a cantina? It's barely past breakfast."

"Sniffing a trail."

"What?"

Slim downed his shot of tequila and walked out to the sidewalk. "Our boys might have stopped here on their way south."

"Not if Digby didn't."

"He might have."

"Bullshit. We hacked into his e-mail. He was heading for Tres Virgenes. Followed by those two goons I hired. Those shit-for-brains were supposed to watch and report back, not steal the goddamned treasure."

"Tortoise wins the race."

"What's that supposed to mean?"

"It means relax. I know what everyone's driving. I know what they look like. Baja's nothing but a small town stretching all the way to Cabo. The road may be paved, but it's like the Wild West down here. People notice things. Like a couple of rednecks following an Indiana Jones wannabe."

"Stay out of the bars and find me that treasure."

"Roger that."

Slim slipped free the earpiece and reentered Hussong's. The sawdust floor smelled inviting, the smoky air reassuring. The mariachi band had finished their song and was regrouping near a table of fresh-faced college kids slamming Cuervo Gold. Slim reclaimed his seat at the bar and removed his cowboy hat.

"Tequila," he said. "*Con sangrita.*"

CHAPTER NINE

Cabo San Lucas, Baja California Sur

Charlie Diamond couldn't believe his good fortune. Thirty minutes after entering Cabo Wabo, not one but two women offered him drinks. Both wore wedding rings and said they were on vacation from their deadbeat husbands back in Detroit. The dark-haired woman wore a miniskirt with a sheer blouse and sandals laced up her ankles and tied midcalf. The platinum blonde cropped her hair into a sexy, androgynous Annie Lennox style. She wore tattered jeans and a black V-neck T-shirt. Both looked to be in their midthirties.

Charlie told them he owned real estate in Detroit—one of the few truths he'd spoken since entering the bar. As the self-described billboard king, Charlie owned square footage in every state in the union. Highway frontage mostly. Small plots of barren earth that spawned advertising eyesores from coast to coast. Locations worth millions. The women were impressed.

"And we've expanded into Mexico," Charlie boasted.

"You have?" the women said excitedly.

Charlie downed his Cape Cod and bent close to his audience. In a loud whisper he said, "I got the exclusive for the Pink Octopus. The owner's a friend of mine. Eccentric art collector named Barbie. Gal's a genius. A fucking weirdo, but brilliant. To be honest, though, she should have named it the Pink Clam, if you know what I mean."

He winked.

The women gave blank stares.

"Cabo's most famous nightclub. It's right around the corner. Gorgeous women dancing all night long."

"I love to dance," said the blonde.

A waitress, in what looked like a Sammy Hagar wig, walked by and Charlie ordered another round of drinks. A pause in the music allowed him to ask the women's names, but before they could answer, "Why Can't This Be Love" blared through the speakers. Charlie felt hands grip both of his elbows, and suddenly he was on the dance floor surrounded by gyrating tourists. He bounced and swayed with one eye on the two women and one eye on the wig-wearing waitress. The moment the drinks arrived he darted to the table with a fistful of twenties and ordered another round. When the song ended the two women returned, slightly out of breath.

"Hey, you cheated," the dark-haired woman protested as the extra drinks arrived. "But thanks for the drinks."

"Hey, you want to see my yachts?" Charlie slurred as the DJ spun a live version of "I Can't Drive 55." He chugged one of his Cape Cods.

"Yachts?" both women blurted in tandem. "As in plural?"

Ten minutes later they stood on the back deck of the *Queen of Diamonds* while Charlie hurried inside for refreshments. He ran a quick check of the remote cameras strategically placed around the master stateroom. One lens was hidden in a taxidermied sailfish eye, another in an air-conditioning vent on the ceiling.

"Three double Cape Cods," Charlie said cheerfully as he returned from the saloon.

"Can you show us around the boat?" the blonde asked.

"Twist my boat-captain arm," he chortled and led them inside. He was making a beeline for the bedroom when one of the women stopped and pointed at a miniature statue of a naked Indian.

"What *is* that?" she asked.

"Mayan porn," Charlie said. "Want to see the master stateroom?"

"More Mayan porn?" asked the other woman.

Both women giggled.

The blonde pointed at a mask hanging from the wall. "Is that real gold?"

"Fourteen-karat," Charlie boasted.

"And the eyes?"

"Diamonds."

The women's eyes widened.

Charlie grinned. "Just wait until you see the bedroom."

"More diamonds?" they asked in tandem.

"See for yourself."

Charlie led them into the bedroom and described the various works of art. As the women ogled the gem-encrusted cloak of an Aztec god, he freed a condom from his pocket and surreptitiously placed it on the bedside table.

"Freshen your drinks?"

"Only if you freshen yours," said the blonde.

As Charlie hurried from the stateroom, the blonde added, "Do you have any robes on board?"

Charlie skidded to a stop. "Robes?"

"You know, bathrobes? I feel like a shower."

"In the closet next to the headboard. Take your pick."

The blonde smiled. "Perfect."

As Charlie resumed his cocktail crusade, the blonde turned to her friend and winked. "Money in the bank, baby."

CHAPTER TEN

Magdalena Bay, Baja California Sur

After the successful night of submarine sabotage, Fish took a short nap aboard his refurbished trawler, and then flew to his sand dune island fifty miles north of the main bay. He fed his Labrador retrievers, Sting and Ray, and then took his rare Appaloosa mule, Mephistopheles, for a ride down the ten-mile beach. The wind had risen with the sun and now the first rays of light illuminated a rolling Pacific that stretched to the horizon like corrugated slate. Fish stopped the mule and scanned the endless vista.

Not much had changed in the years since he'd purchased Isla Santo Domingo, a ten-mile-long sand dune shaped like a scythe. It was one link of a sandy chain of barrier islands protecting Magdalena Bay from the Pacific Ocean six hundred miles south of San Diego. Fish had bought the island twelve years earlier, after fleeing south by seaplane with millions in cash and gems hidden in the plane's belly.

The sparse beauty of the sand dunes had intrigued him, as had the labyrinth of mangroves and the dearth of meddling tourists. The relative proximity of the port town of San Carlos, fifty miles to the south, was also a plus. Close enough to fly his seaplane or drive his panga, yet far enough away for the solitude an expatriate with a world-class secret required. A place to hide some of his fortune, build his fortress, and avoid the fanatics who wanted him dead.

Fish adjusted his mullet-skin cap and fingered the metal fishing crimp holding the tip of his goatee. The chin-tail was wavy and bleached from years of seaside living. He wore a guayabera opened to the waist and a pair of lightweight dungarees. Haulms of sun-washed hair brushed the tops of his broad shoulders. It was mid-June and soon the air would blaze like a welder's torch. But at the moment, dawn was pleasant and the upwelling of the Pacific added a briny coolness to the breeze. He turned Mephistopheles and gently heeled the mule down the sand when an explosion split the serenity like a sonic boom.

A second explosion quickly followed, sending Fish and his mule southward at a near-gallop. With one hand held firmly to Mephistopheles's mane, Fish reached down with the other and loosened the machete strapped to his thigh. Next he opened one of the two saddlebags draped over the mule's withers and felt for the Armamex pistol lying beneath a canteen of water, miscellaneous fishing supplies, and a small bowie knife. He maneuvered the pistol to the top of the bag's leather flap, hoping it was an unnecessary precaution.

A third explosion changed his mind and he pulled the gun free. Fish had never owned a firearm up north. Never needed one. Preferring instead to use persuasion, or if needed, his signature haymaker. Fish had once been a Golden Gloves boxer in college with a promising future when a bad decision on a motorcycle nearly cost him a leg. Unable to train, Fish focused on graduating and took the LSAT on a lark. An inordinately high score led to law school and a career as a trial attorney. The courtroom replaced the boxing ring, and for fifteen years legalese seemed a safe alternative to pugilism.

But trouble had a way of riffling the waters of his life. Even isolated on a remote sand dune island with a new name in a new country, Fish knew his secret couldn't last, knew the crazies would eventually close in.

Now, as he looked over the last rise of sand before Boca de Santo Domingo, where the incoming tide allowed small boats a brief passage twice a day, he spotted the outlines of two men and a beached inflatable dinghy. The dinghy was heavily patched, covered in Confederate flag decals, and carried a corroded outboard motor permanently affixed to the stern. The engine cowling was missing and a frayed starter cord hung limply over the side. The strangers stood on the shoreline, holding rifles aimed over the sea. A plastic cooler with a broken top sat on the sand beside a pile of dead birds. Beyond that were half a dozen cans glinting brightly in the sun.

Beer cans.

Budweiser.

Fish nudged Mephistopheles faster.

"*Compas*," he called out, keeping the pistol hidden in his lap.

The two men whirled toward him with weapons raised.

Fish held up his free hand. "Whoa, now."

"Jesus, you're American?" said the heavyset one in a deep Texas drawl. He wore a cowboy hat, tight jeans, and work boots, and looked no older than twenty. He squatted down and plucked a can of Budweiser from the sand.

Fish lowered his hand. "Heck of a morning."

"Damn straight," the thinner man agreed. He also wore a cowboy hat, jeans, and boots. He and the fat man were shirtless, with stark farmer tans.

"How'd you get the guns across the border?"

The fat man sneered. "Inside a bag of Costco dog chow. Mexicans ain't the smartest beans in the burrito."

The skinny man sniggered.

"You smuggled .22's into Baja to shoot a bunch of seabirds?" Fish continued.

"Hell no," the skinny man explained. "Brought 'em for protection against the drug lords. Ain't none around so we're headed for Cabo to check out the topless chicks."

"Seems you made a wrong turn."

"Naw," the skinny man said, shaking his head. "Moose here heard about some weirdo bar with a bunch of drunken iguanas.

Supposed to have the coldest beer in Baja. Checked it out before heading out here to blow some shit up."

"Didn't think much of the bar?" Fish asked, his sea-green eyes flickering between fascination and revulsion.

The fat man named Moose chimed in. "Wasn't bad. Only saw one iguana, though. And it wasn't even drunk. Didn't have no Bud neither. Cold goddamn Coronas, I'll give 'em that. But the jukebox sucked. Could've used some Jerry Jeff. More Waylon, for sure. Hell, there wasn't even a David Allan Coe on the whole list."

Fish rubbed out a chain of sweat working its way down his neck and scanned the surrounding carnage. "You planning to camp here tonight?"

"You crazy?" Moose scoffed. "Too danged hot. Got us a shade tree across the bay. Pickup's full of ice and Budweiser."

"I heard explosions."

"M-80's. Stork here lights 'em. I throw 'em. Quarter stick of dynamite works a hell of a lot better on the big birds. Been blowing pelicans right out of the sky. Got another one a few minutes ago." He high-fived the skinnier man. "Alamo should be bringing it back any minute. Meanwhile, we're hoping another dumbass gull drops by for a visit."

"Alamo?"

"Pit bull," Stork interjected. "Loves to chase shit. Moose here used to pitch in high school. Now he's a dog trainer."

The fat man nodded and did his best Nolan Ryan with the empty Budweiser can. It twirled anemically through the air and dropped to the sand. "Beer me, bro."

Stork opened the cooler and fished out a fresh can. He glanced up at Fish. "Want one, mister?"

Fish shook his head. He pointed a finger at the pile of seagulls lying near the dinghy. "What happened to the gulls?"

"Walked right up and shot 'em. Hell, they ain't even afraid of humans."

"They are now," Stork snorted.

"You planning to eat them?"

Moose let out a laugh. "Riding that old donkey with no saddle's jumbled your brains, mister. Gulls ain't nothing but rats with feathers."

"She's a mule."

"Don't make a rat's ass to me."

"The gulls or the mule?"

Moose blinked vapidly.

Fish tugged at his braided goatee. "I hate to see something so pretty go to such waste."

"Pretty fucking annoying is more like it," Moose said, and chugged the entire Budweiser. He crumpled it in his hand and heaved it toward the sand dunes. "How'd you learn to speak Mexican?"

"Spanish."

"Huh?"

"Hey, here comes Alamo!" Stork yelled and hurried toward the water. An exhausted pit bull with a heavy chain and padlock hung around its neck emerged from the waves with a dead pelican in its teeth.

"Good boy," Stork said and rubbed the dog's head.

The dog dropped the pelican to the sand and slumped to his haunches, panting hard, a line of white foam encircling its mouth.

Fish tilted back his cap. "Your dog's dehydrated."

"Who, Alamo?" Moose asked. "Hell, he can swim all day and still hump a bitch coyote."

The two friends chest-bumped with a tandem "Hell yeah!" that sent Stork rebounding backward. He tripped over a beer can and fell flat to the sand.

"Your dog's going to drown with that chain around his neck," Fish said.

Moose dug through the cooler for another beer. "Drown? Hell, with a neck the size of a pony keg, he don't even know it's there anymore. Here, watch this."

Moose cocked his arm and flung the full beer into the water beyond the breakers. "Fetch, boy!"

As Stork stood to wipe sand from his pants, the pit bull leapt to its feet and bounded into the surf. It struggled through the breakers and began to circle the rolling swells twenty yards from shore.

"Moose?" Stork asked sheepishly as his friend opened a fresh beer. "Does Budweiser float?"

"Huh?"

"I think Alamo just dove under to try and find it on the bottom."

Moose stared blankly across the waves when his head jerked up. "Crow!"

Both men raised their rifles and began firing at a frigate bird gliding overhead.

Fish dropped the Armamex into the saddlebag, dismounted, and took two quick steps across the sand disarming both shooters with fists to the kidneys. He followed up with swift right jabs to the solar plexus. As the two men lay gasping for breath, Fish flung the .22's into the sea. He spotted the pit bull thrashing where it had disappeared moments earlier, turned, and hurried back to the saddlebags. He retrieved a spool of fishing line and the knife, and trussed the men's arms tightly in front of them. He removed their hats, boots, and socks, and then cut their remaining clothes loose and tossed everything into the dinghy.

As their breath returned, Moose said, "You fucking gay or something? Give us back our clothes!"

Fish ignored him. He hustled to Mephistopheles and rummaged through the second saddlebag for a roll of duct tape. Then he pulled the dinghy into the sea.

"Hey, that's my boat!"

Fish slid it beyond the breakers and climbed aboard.

"You can't leave us out here. It's hot and there ain't no shade!"

"You've got a cooler full of melting ice," Fish said and started the outboard motor. "Use it to stay hydrated." He tossed the roll of duct tape to the sand. "As for shade, I suggest you put those feathered rats to good use."

Moose spat into the sand. "I ain't taping no dead birds on no naked guy."

"Suit yourself," Fish said and roared toward the spot where Alamo had once again disappeared beneath the waves.

CHAPTER ELEVEN

Cabo San Lucas, Baja California Sur

Charlie Diamond felt the yacht sway with the weight of a visitor. He'd been futilely attempting to break free of his restraints since awakening with a crushing headache and a vague memory of "one last shot" before allowing the two women to strip him and tie him to the bed with sashes from his loaner bathrobes. He knew he was in trouble when the platinum blonde shoved one of his socks into his mouth and secured it with the final sash.

Now as he craned his neck, he cringed at the sight of his nakedness. Written in lipstick across his torso was a directive: *Wink into the fish eye, Charlie. Talk soon.*

Charlie glanced up at the wall where the stuffed sailfish hung askew. The small hole drilled strategically behind the glass eye was empty of its wires. Charlie craned his neck toward the small bureau beside the bed. The top drawer was pulled out, the video recorder missing.

Charlie struggled against the wraps binding his arms and legs to the bedposts. Four of his favorite bathrobes now hung from each post. The fifth lay in a bundle by the door. Charlie screamed into the sock gagging his mouth. The yacht swayed. Charlie prayed it wasn't the two women returning to torture him.

As the footfalls approached the door to the master stateroom, Charlie clamped his eyes shut. Sunlight flooded the room.

"*Ay, caramba!*" Charlie's maid shrieked.

Charlie opened his eyes.

The maid shook her finger angrily. "*Señor Diamond, usted portar mal anoche!*"

Charlie nodded. He motioned an appeal for forgiveness with his eyes and flapped his arms and legs against the bed.

"*Lo suelto?*" she asked scornfully and opened the window blinds.

Charlie squinted painfully at the sunlight and heard his cell phone ring from the back deck.

The maid saw the look of expectation on Charlie's face. "No good talking with *un calcetín* in your mouth, no?"

Charlie stopped nodding and felt suddenly nauseous.

The maid let out a shriek. "Your art?" she said, and walked around the room inspecting the vacant walls and empty end tables. "*Donde está?*"

Charlie's eyes fluttered in shock. He groaned loudly into the sock double-knotted around his jaw.

"I tell you one thing, Señor Diamond, you mess with the wrong señoritas this time."

Charlie screamed into his gag. He flapped his hands and made cutting motions with his fingers.

"*Tijeras?*"

Charlie nodded frantically.

The maid disappeared into the galley and returned seconds later with a large steak knife. "No scissors," she said. "*El cuchillo es mejor.* You much too old for such games as this. Maybe I help you quit this nonsense." She jabbed the knife toward his manhood.

Charlie screeched.

"Hombres," she scoffed, reaching out to slit the binds from Charlie's legs. Then she walked to the head of the bed and cut the binds from his wrists.

Charlie scudded to the side of the bed. He yanked the sash from his face, spit out the sock, and raced to the back deck to retrieve his cell phone and check the messages.

The maid glanced around the room, her eyes pausing on the bureau and its open top drawer. She tossed the knife to the floor and allowed a brief smile to flood her face with joy.

"*Que se va*," she cooed, and walked through the bedroom's side door to the back deck, picking up the pace as she disappeared up the dock.

CHAPTER TWELVE

Magdalena Bay, Baja California Sur

After leaving the bird killers naked on the beach, Atticus Fish sent Mephistopheles home with a sharp whistle, as he circled the water where the pit bull had disappeared for the second time. He spotted the dog five feet below the surface, its legs slowing, its eyes closing. He dived overboard, caught the heavy padlock hanging from its neck, and returned the drowning animal to the surface. He swam the weakened dog to the dinghy and hauled it inside, and minutes later motored through Boca de Santo Domingo and across the bay to the bird killers' campsite. The lopsided Army tent hidden between a set of mangroves was the first clue. The Confederate flag draped across the back window of a nearby red-white-and-blue Dodge Ram was a dead giveaway.

He carried the dog ashore and placed it in the shade of a mesquite tree, rummaged the campsite for water and dog food, and then packed up the tent and loaded it into the bed of the truck. As the dog lapped water from a dented hubcap, Fish used a large stone to smash the truck's passenger-side window. He slid the seat forward and removed a heavy-duty toolbox from the floorboard. He dumped the contents to the ground and found a rusty hacksaw.

Minutes later the chain fell from the dog's neck. Fish hurled it into the dinghy. Next he removed the Texas license plate from the front bumper, refilled the dog's water, and then boarded the dinghy. He took the long way back, motoring through a labyrinth of mangroves checking half a dozen shrimp traps. He had time to kill before returning to the bird killers. Hours of free time before flying to La Paz to confront the infamous Ronald Stump. Hours for the morning sun to rise overhead and teach his captives a lesson. Burn a little sense into them.

As he rounded a thick copse of mangrove, he spotted Baja's preeminent mescal salesman and ironwood carving counterfeiter, Skegs. The nearly six-foot-tall Seri Indian wore wraparound shades and a long-billed fishing cap. He was unusually tall for a Seri, and had denim-colored eyes and a nest of hair that hung from his head like seaweed.

Skegs stood at the stern of a familiar twenty-two-foot aluminum Gregor, leaning against its Evinrude outboard, the stainless-steel propeller locked safely above the marled bottom. A wannabe world-class fisherman, Skegs wore an AFTCO fishing shirt emblazoned with leaping wahoos, and a pair of matching Bluewater fishing shorts. In his right hand was an Abu-Garcia graphite fishing rod. His left hand held the throttle of a 36-volt electric trolling motor. He looked up at the sound of the approaching outboard.

"Nice boat," Skegs called out as Fish sidled up beside him. "Steal it from a hobo?"

"On loan, so to speak."

"Getting skunked swordfishing last night was a drag. I hope you don't mind me borrowing your boat. Isabela gave me the keys."

"Anytime."

"I thought about tossing your crappy fishing stuff overboard. You know, to try and get the stink off the boat."

"Uh-huh."

"I figured this would do the job instead." He opened the lid of an SKB-7200 tackle box, his blue eyes dancing over the array of color-coded lures. "About time you showed up. The tide's already halfway in."

"Had to disarm a couple of cowboys."

"That explains all those Confederate flag stickers." He reached down between the seats and passed Fish a ramshackle rod with a tarnished Penn reel and a shoebox of homemade lures. "Good luck catching anything with that."

"Luck's got nothing to do with it."

"These cowboys—were they after your money or your head?"

"Neither."

Skegs lowered his sunglasses. "Do tell."

Fish shrugged. "Couple of hicks taking potshots at pelicans. Killed half a dozen gulls, too. Almost got a frigate."

"What is it with gringos and their guns? Seems like every white guy's got one these days."

"Texans. Drunk on Budweiser. Driving a red-white-and-blue pickup with a Confederate flag hanging from the back window. A real piece of work, those two."

Skegs shoved his sunglasses back in place. "Maybe we should introduce them to a little local intervention? Xavier says he's got a couple of badasses in jail. Guaranteed to open up a *ballena* of whoopass on some good old boys from Texas."

"I got it covered." Fish held up a feathered 1/16-ounce jig head with a bituminous tail.

"Seriously, Sandman. You need to update your gear."

Fish didn't respond. Instead he tied the jig straight to the end of a length of yellowing monofilament line, and then turned his attention to the swirl of water ebbing around the exposed roots of a thick mangrove bush.

"No swivel?" Skegs asked, more critical than curious.

"Distracts from the presentation."

"You call *that* a presentation?" Skegs slid open a drawer of his tackle box and removed a shiny red barrel swivel. "This bright red stimulates the feeding instincts of game fish by imitating a wounded bait," he explained before Fish could ask.

Fish checked the sharpness of the hook with his thumb. "Speaking of imitations, I need more ironwood. The drunken iguanas are especially popular with the bar crowd."

"Just so happens I dropped a case back at the bar. Fresh batch of mescal, too."

Fish relayed his appreciation with a nod.

Skegs carefully tied the swivel to the end of his neon pink fishing line. "This new line's dope. Totally undetectable. Scientifically tested. Had a hit right before you showed up."

"Sure it wasn't a snag?"

"That's just rude, man. You show up late in a stolen dinghy, and now you're an expert in all things snooky?"

"Snooky?" Fish asked, his green eyes flashing at the thought of Baja's legendary black snook. The near mythical fish had been targeted without success by some of the world's best fishermen. Other than a few local *pangeros*, and the expatriate with the homemade lures, no one had ever landed one.

"You got any black rubber bands in that suitcase?" Fish asked as he smoothed the frigate feathers over the shaft of the small, barbless hook.

"You color-blind? The water's all stirred up with the tide. No self-respecting snook's going to touch that thing without some color. I'm beginning to think all those once-in-a-lifetime catches were flukes."

"A fluke?" Fish let out a laugh. "That's a good one. I didn't think you had it in you."

"Ah, man. There you go again. Who says Indians can't be funny? John Belushi was funny. Bet you didn't know he was part Indian."

Fish shot him a questioning look.

"Yeah, man. Chickasaw. On his mother's side."

"Is that so?" Fish feigned interest.

"Wouldn't lie about a thing like that," Skegs said and held out a bright-red rubber band. "Here's a little something to give that lure thing of yours a chance."

Fish waved it off. He pitched the feathered hook into the current and let it glide beneath the mangrove roots. As he twitched the rod tip, Skegs pulled out a rack of expensive lures.

"Time to get schooled," Skegs said and held up a shiny holographic version of a baitfish. He clipped the chartreuse Yozuri Crystal Minnow Floater to the red swivel hanging from the end of the bright-pink fishing line.

"You'll scare all the fish away."

"Snook are some of the shyest fish in the sea. Pink's the most invisible. Got to evolve with the times, amigo. Today's fish are smarter than they used to be."

"Unlike today's anglers, apparently."

Skegs ignored the insult and added a bright-red split-shot weight to the front of the barrel swivel. He admired the presentation and then flipped the lure into the air, its mirrored sides flashing like a disco ball. The lure landed in the current and sank.

"Shouldn't take long," Skegs said, and cranked the handle on a brand new black-and-red spinning reel with yellow flame decals.

"Star Wars convention?" Fish asked, eyeing the patterned reel.

"Top-of-the-line Shimano Torque. Only six hundred bucks. Picked it up last week down at Minerva's. Put the decals on myself."

"Six hundred bucks? Mescal business must be booming."

"Never thought I'd say it, but La Paz is turning into a mini-Cabo. Taking a run at all the tourists. Three new golf courses, couple new marinas, bars popping out like whiteheads. I can barely keep up with the place."

Fish pointed out at the water. "Looks like your fancy lure's attracting more than fish." He retrieved his lure and made a second cast.

Skegs scowled as he brought the tangled lure to the boat and shook free a strand of seaweed. He pitched the lure to the far side of the channel and reeled faster. Nothing. He reared back and flung the offering far down the center of the channel. As it soared through the air, a gust of wind carried it into a bramble of mangroves. The clattering snag sent a great blue heron squawking skyward.

"Damn," Skegs complained.

He had just reversed the trolling motor to retrieve his treed lure when Fish's antique Penn Senator rang out with a strike and the homemade fishing rod slumped forward. The water swirled with the wide sweep of a tail, and then exploded with the head of a large black snook. The fish lingered at the surface as if curious about its pursuer before surging for the maze of underwater roots. Fish bent forward and drove the tip of the rod toward the muddy bottom. He snapped his wrists, jackknifing the rod tip and turning the snook away from its hiding place and back toward the channel.

"I think you snagged it," Skegs commented. "Looked foul-hooked when it surfaced."

"Grab the net. He's coming up again."

Skegs set his rod and reel to the boat's stern, and slipped the net from its holder beneath the gunwale. He dipped it into the muddy water and watched Fish maneuver an eight-pound black snook into the mesh. The two boats drifted together and Fish reached down and removed the hook from the snook's jaw.

"Weird place for a snag," Fish said. He removed an iPhone from his pocket and snapped photos of the netted snook.

"Happens," Skegs muttered.

"Hold it up so I can get a better shot."

"It's your fish. You hold it up."

"You're more photogenic."

"You can say that again." Skegs reached into the net and removed the fish. "I still say you snagged it."

Fish took a series of photos and pocketed the phone. "Toss him back."

"Are you nuts? This is the rarest fish in Baja."

"Which is why I'm letting it go."

"Nobody's going to believe you."

"We have the photos."

"They'll say you faked it."

"Fine with me."

"But—"

"Uh-oh," Fish said and gazed over his friend's head.

Skegs spun around.

"Shoo!" the mescal salesman hollered. He heaved the snook football-style toward a snowy egret eyeing the holographic lure hanging from the branches. The snook splashed harmlessly into the water and swam away. The egret snatched the lure in its beak and flapped its wings.

"No!" Skegs screamed and watched his Abu-Garcia graphite fishing rod rocket from the gunwale, its aeronautical shaft whizzing across the surface like an elongated missile.

CHAPTER THIRTEEN

Punta Baja, Baja California Sur

"Man, I'm beat," Zack said with a yawn as he climbed up the rocky beach, seawater dripping from his ginger-colored beard.

He and his twin brother Jack had spent most of the night hauling the trunk of Jesuit Treasure down the canyon. They'd freed Digby's Ford-150 from the sand, and then loaded the heavy cache into the truck bed between the outboard motor and the fishing equipment. Then they split up, with Jack driving their 1979 Toyota short-bed pickup, and Zack following behind in Digby's F-150 with the professor and the treasure.

The men avoided pavement and instead took a dry arroyo to the rugged coastline at Punta Baja. Miles from civilization, the rocky beach housed the cardboard remnants of an abandoned fish camp and the skeletal remains of a beaked whale. Rocky cliffs protected the small beach where a poorly marked dirt path led to a cave that overlooked the sea.

Now, as Zack sat on a rock staring absently at the Sea of Cortez, he said, "One of us has to keep an eye on Indiana Jones over there." He pointed at the truck where Digby snored loudly.

"Think he's faking it?" Jack asked. He wedged a fat marble of Copenhagen into his bottom lip.

"Won't matter if your knot holds."

"It'll hold."

"I'm taking a nap."

"Why you and not me?"

"Because I'm the oldest. Go take a swim. It'll wake you up."

Jack spat onto the rocks. "You just swam and now you're taking a nap."

"Exactly." Zack stretched out on the warm rock.

"Fine. Sleep. I'm going to take a crack at catching us dinner. There's fishing gear in the bed of his truck."

"Have at it, Ahab."

Jack narrowed his gaze. "I ain't no A-rab."

"Not A-*rab*, A-*hab*. The guy from the movie, dimwit. He tried to catch a big white whale. But the whale was such a badass it sunk his boat and bit off his leg."

"You sure it wasn't a shark?"

"I'm sure."

"Whales ain't got teeth."

"This one did."

"Sounds made up."

"The one-legged dude was a fisherman."

Jack scratched at a stalk of greasy hair and spat. "I can catch a fish."

"Maybe from a supermarket."

"You'll see."

Zack stretched out on the rock, the sound of the lapping waves leadening his eyelids. He slid his Dodgers cap over his face. "Wake me in a couple hours. We'll share a can of ravioli."

Jack scowled. He pulled his Angels cap down low and walked to Digby's truck, where he removed the surf rod poking out between cases of beer. The archaeology professor continued to snore. Jack gently opened the lid of the ancient trunk and pocketed a gold peso. Then he rummaged around and found the tackle box. Minutes later the kidnapper stood in ankle-deep water casting a heavy metal lure into the light surf. It was early afternoon and the June sun was like a bonfire overhead.

Jack made a few anemic casts before launching the lure far from the shore. He cranked the handle on the spinning reel and felt a sudden resistance on the line. He reared back and heard the reel clatter like cards in the spokes of a wheel.

"Holy shit!" he hollered, splashing into deeper water.

Digby stopped snoring. Zack lifted his cap and opened a heavy eye.

Jack slipped and fell face first into the water, losing his baseball cap. He emerged gasping for air, the fishing rod still spitting line.

"Hey, I think I caught something!"

Digby stepped from the passenger side of his truck, his hands still trussed in front of him, and wandered toward the shoreline. "Could be a halibut."

"I like halibut," Jack said, and began to reel in line. "Big, round, flat things, right?"

"Right."

Jack stopped reeling and eyed Digby suspiciously. "You ain't trying to escape are you?"

Digby held out his trussed hands. "And miss all the fun?"

Jack didn't answer. He turned back and reeled, and soon saw a flat round fish glide exhaustedly into view. He reached down, grasped it by its toothless mouth, and hefted it into the air.

"Zack, I got us a halibut for dinner!"

Digby stepped forward. "You might want to be careful—"

"Don't come any closer!" Jack hollered. He raised the fish over his head like a weapon. It flapped its wings once, then whipped its tail across Jack's face. Jack dropped the fish and screamed.

Zack jumped to his feet and raced across the beach, his gun in his outstretched hand.

"What the hell just happened?"

Digby shrugged. "I told him to be careful."

"Jack, you all right?" his brother asked.

Jack was on his knees, his face in his hands.

"Jack, can you hear me?!"

Jack nodded, blood threading his fingers and drenching his beard. "The halibut bit me in the face," he blubbered. "I think my eye's busted or something. I can't see nothing."

"It wasn't a halibut," Digby said, carefully unhooking the fish from the lure with his roped hands.

"But it was big and flat like you said," Jack blubbered, dropping his hands from his face.

"So's a stingray."

"Mother of God," Zack said and looked away.

Digby leaned down and inspected the wound. "We need to get him to a hospital."

"No way," Zack said.

"He just got whacked in the eye by a ray. There's venom in that barb. It'll get infected if it's not treated. He could lose his eye. Or worse."

"Then clean the wound," Zack said. "We're not leaving until I say we're leaving."

"It's swollen shut."

"He's got another eye."

"You're kidding!"

Zack aimed the gun at the stingray and fired. "You're the one who said it was a halibut." The gun angled upward toward Digby's chest. "You better fix him, Professor. If you ever want to see home again."

CHAPTER FOURTEEN

Magdalena Bay, Baja California Sur

After leaving Skegs in search of the snowy egret towing the expensive Abu-Garcia fishing rod, Fish returned to his island and the bird killers. It was nearing noon and the rising tide allowed easy passage through Boca de Santo Domingo.

Fish beached the dinghy and stepped barefoot to the sand. The fat man named Moose was facedown and surrounded by dozens of beer cans. His backside glowed like a burning coal beneath a blanket of dead seagulls. The skinny man named Stork sat hunched on the overturned ice chest, his head hung low, his knees tucked to his chest. The beak of the dead pelican was duct-taped to his head, its wingspan stretched and taped to his back.

Fish strode up to the pair and tipped his mullet-skin cap. "Howdy boys."

Stork jerked upright and tumbled to the sand. He let out a yelp and scrambled back atop the cooler. "Beach is hotter than a Walmart parking lot. How can you stand there with no shoes on?"

"Practice."

"You live here?"

"I like the neighborhood."

"You ain't scared of getting mugged by the locals?"

Fish ignored the question. He noticed Moose shivering in the triple-digit heat. "How much water did he drink?"

"None."

"None?"

"Said it was swimming with parasites and shit. He pissed in it to make sure I didn't drink none."

"It's not parasites that scare me. It's goons with guns and less sense than the gulls they're shooting at. Get in the skiff."

"You going to kill us?"

"Tempting."

"I think Moose's already dead."

"He's alive."

"His back is toast. I had to wait for him to pass out before I could cover him with birds."

"You do everything Moose tells you?"

Stork shrugged. "He's got a GED. Even took some classes at El Paso Community College. Hey, are you really one of those human rights whackos that leaves water in the desert for them aliens?"

Fish scooped Moose from the sand, carried him to the dinghy, and dropped him inside.

Moose blinked his eyes groggily. "Water," he moaned.

"You shouldn't have pissed in it," Fish said. He motioned for Stork to join them in the dinghy.

"No way. Sand's too hot."

"You stay here much longer and you'll die of dehydration."

Stork shrugged again.

Fish pushed the boat into the surf and started the outboard. As he gunned the engine he heard screams and turned to see Stork sprinting across the sand. The skinny American belly-flopped into the water and grabbed the edge of the inflatable with his tied hands. Fish reached over and hauled him aboard. Ten minutes later they slid ashore near the old red pickup. Alamo had regained his strength and barked happily at their arrival.

Fish turned to Stork. "Put your friend in the truck and drive home."

"Naked?"

"Your clothes are in the front seat. Along with cash for the boat and outboard."

"You're taking our boat?"

"Donating it to the local sea turtle sanctuary."

"Moose's gonna be pissed."

"You tell Moose if I ever see him again he'll be more than pissed. He'll be sitting in a Mexican jail. Killing seabirds is against the law in this country. Not to mention cruel and senseless."

Stork gave a weak nod and stepped to the rocky shore. He fell to his knees and cried out. "My feet are blistered bad. I can't walk."

"Those aliens you spoke about earlier. The ones dying of thirst in the middle of the desert? They walk for miles on blistered feet. Without a cool ocean breeze or a cooler of water to piss in. And the ones who don't die of exposure end up working in triple-digit heat so you and Bullwinkle can buy cheap strawberries and cotton T-shirts with cartoon logos."

Moose sat up glassy-eyed and said, "What'd you call me?"

"Get out."

Moose looped a weak fist at Fish, who caught it midflight. He pushed against Moose's outstretched arm and watched the overweight man topple over the bow and land on his sunburned back.

"Ahhh...!"

Moose rolled to his stomach and struggled to his knees swaying drunkenly. "You're a dead man, mister."

Fish turned his attention to Stork, who was crabbing away on his hands and knees. "I cut the chain from Alamo's neck. If you care one wit about that dog, you'll keep it that way. I also removed the front license plate from your truck. If you're not across the border by tomorrow my friends in law enforcement will know. You think today was bad, stick around for the encore."

Fish slid the boat into deeper water and without another word sped toward his seaplane moored near his house across the bay. He had promised Toozie he'd be in La Paz before Ronald Stump left for Cabo San Lucas. Have a little chat with the meddling real estate mogul.

Hand the tycoon a million-dollar incentive to stay the hell out of Magdalena Bay.

CHAPTER FIFTEEN

Baja California Norte

Slim Dixon steadied his arm on the driver-side door of the grey 1960 convertible Cadillac and aimed a Beretta M9 at a wake of vultures clustered around a dead and bloated cow. He slowed the car and pulled the trigger and watched the sky turn black with birds. Then he watched the vultures circle briefly before alighting around their fallen comrade, tearing into its warm flesh.

"Loyal sonsabitches," he remarked and tossed the pistol to the passenger seat.

After drinking all morning at Hussong's in Ensenada, Slim had driven through the afternoon, stopping at various Pemex gas stations to inquire about the southbound Americans. One gas station attendant remembered a truck with Arizona plates and an aluminum skiff on the rack, but not the twin brothers. Another attendant remembered the twins but not the archaeologist. Slim didn't really care. But for smashing into a wayward cow or a ubiquitous semi swerving into their paths, both trucks would have made it into the Tres Virgenes. Once there, the archaeologist would have found the treasure and the twins would have stolen it. The question was, *where were they now?*

Slim drove his old Cadillac into the town of El Rosario and pulled onto the dirt lot of Mama Espinoza's. He needed a drink. Maybe a grilled lobster tail chunked small and rolled into a fresh-baked tortilla. A hefty slather of real Mexican hot sauce and a bottle of Corona. Maybe a few bottles. Catch a few hours of sleep in the Cadillac before heading inland and driving through the night. The twins wouldn't be far. Not with all that loot. They'd be indecisive. Scared. And soon they'd be dead. The archaeologist, too, if he wasn't already.

Slim had just stepped from the car when the sound of squealing tires startled him. He spun on his cowboy boots as a jacked-up shiny black Chevy Silverado with Mexican plates and oversize Dually wheels fishtailed across the roadway and clipped the back end of the Cadillac. The young driver wore a San Diego Chargers baseball cap and a pair of dark sunglasses. A pretty señorita snuggled against him, his arm draped around her neck.

As the truck rebounded from the Cadillac, Slim noticed the bulbous rubber sack resembling a bull's scrotum swinging from the hitch that extended from the chrome bumper. He heard a popular *narcocorrido* tune blasting from the open driver-side window.

The young Mexican man regained control of the truck and flung an empty Dos Equis bottle out the window. It shattered on the pavement in a spray of green glitter. The truck ran the stop sign at the corner, turned left, and disappeared.

Slim glanced back at the restaurant and the large, hand-painted sign beside the front door. It read, in English, LOBSTER BURRITOS. A second sign read *Hielo Purificado y Cerveza Fría.*

Slim removed his cowboy hat and rubbed out a line of sweat pooling at his brow. He walked to the trunk of the Cadillac and ran a long-fingered hand across the crumpled tail fin. Pieces of brake light littered the ground. Slim bent down and plucked a red shard from the dirt. His jaw clenched. He placed the cowboy hat back to his head and straightened it, pocketing the shard of plastic and opening the car door. He backed the Cadillac away from the restaurant.

Finding that shiny black Silverado with a freshly dented front bumper would be easy. Eliminating a narco-trafficker wannabe from the human race wouldn't be hard either.

But leaving Mama Espinoza's and her famous lobster burritos and ice-chilled beer was one of the hardest things he'd done in months.

CHAPTER SIXTEEN

Punta Baja, Baja California Sur

Zack held the gun on Digby as he led the archaeologist and a blubbering twin brother up the dirt path toward the mouth of the cliffside cave. Jack's poisoned eye protruded from his head like a purple cue ball. His cheek puffed out and the skin of his neck was webbed with tendrils of dried blood. The air was pregnant with moisture. Overhead, thunderclouds roiled the afternoon sky.

"This better not be a trick," Zack said and jabbed the barrel into Digby's back.

Digby didn't answer.

"A *chubasco* sounds made up," Jack complained through trembling lips. His voice sounded as if it was pumped through a bag of marbles. "Like Mexican Tabasco or that fried pig stuff."

"*Chicharrónes*," Digby said flatly.

"I loves those things," Jack mumbled and dug out his can of Copenhagen and shoved a plug into his swollen lower lip.

Digby adjusted his wide-brimmed hat and kept walking.

"I've heard of typhoons," Zack chimed in. "And hurricanes and shit. And that tempest in a teapot crap. But I've never heard about this *chubasco* bullshit. You're telling me some badass Mexican storm is about to bring down the great flood? Even if it does, there isn't anything but bone-dry desert out here. Ground's so parched it could soak up the ocean."

Digby stopped at the entrance to the cave. He turned to Zack. "This desert's been baked by the sun for a million years. Hard as concrete. When the *chubasco* hits, that arroyo's going to fill up like a culvert and wash everything away. You better hope our trucks are parked high enough."

"Only one truck I give a damn about. And I already moved it as high as I'm going to." He raised two fingers to his eyes. "Storm or no storm, someone's got to keep an eye on that treasure of ours."

"Don't say I didn't warn you when the artifacts get washed into the surf."

Jack sent a weak stream of tobacco juice into the dirt, and one-eyed his older brother. "He's calling it that again, Zack."

Zack kicked Digby in the knee. "Enough with the artifact mumbo jumbo. It's treasure, goddammit. Stolen from the church by a bunch of double-crossing priests. Now it's ours."

Digby frowned.

Zack kicked him again. "Insult my brother again and I'll shoot your fucking kneecap off. You already messed up his face with that halibut nonsense."

Digby turned. "Please don't kick me again."

Zack allowed a smile to creep across his face. He cocked the trigger and aimed. "Just give me a reason."

Digby turned back and started for the cave. Moments later the trio reached the entrance. Zack stopped, and wagged the gun toward the path at the far side of the opening. "What's that mound of shells doing over there?" he asked suspiciously.

"Midden pile."

"English."

"A pile of oyster shells."

"No way. Ocean's too far away to wash any oysters up here."

"It was Indians, not waves."

Jack spun around, his working eye as wide as a sand dollar. Zack raised the gun again.

Digby brushed at his blond mustache and sighed. "Long dead Indians. Hundreds of years ago. They took shelter in caves like this one."

Zack lowered the gun. "You better not be lying."

"Go see for yourself."

"Some other time."

"I found a pearl once," Jack slurred. He tried to send a ribbon of spit over the pile of shells, but a sudden gust of wind airmailed the saliva over the edge of the cliff. "Inside an oyster. At the Pima County Fair. Cost me five bucks."

"The Indians traded pearls with the priests," Digby said matter-of-factly.

"No shit?" Zack said.

"No shit."

A powerful gust of wind whipped across the dirt path causing Digby to catch his hat before helping Jack toward the cave.

"Whoa, Professor," Zack barked. "Me first."

His brother pursed his lips awkwardly and launched a missile of brown saliva into the cave. Digby pulled him back.

Zack held the gun high and stepped forward. "Nobody's walking us into a trap."

"You're kidding," Digby said.

"You seem to know a hell of a lot about this area."

"Which means what? I hid a weapon inside this cave in case I ever got nabbed by a couple of boneheads and had to take refuge from a storm?"

Zack's face wrinkled into a clench. "Careful."

Digby shrugged.

"How far back's it go?"

"How the hell should I know?"

Zack ducked his head and disappeared into the gloom.

Digby waited a few seconds and then stepped into the cave. "Satisfied?" he called out.

"I can't see a goddamn thing in here. You got any matches?"

A sudden flash of lightening illuminated the blackness and Digby glimpsed a large, hairy shadow shuffling sideways. Thunder roared overhead and raindrops began to batter the rocks and dust. Digby quickly stepped back outside and hauled Jack over to the midden pile, ignoring the rain. The two men crouched behind the shells and waited. Seconds later, a blood-curdling scream emanated from the blackness followed by the explosion of gunpowder and the whine of a ricocheting bullet. A guttural hiss echoed outward and then another scream and a second gunshot.

"Zack?" Jack mumbled.

The silence was broken by the clank of a gun clattering to the rocks. Lightning flashed again, and a large, doglike animal loped from the cave and scrabbled up the cliff, a streak of crimson running down its ringed tail.

"*Mapache grande,*" Digby remarked, his voice tinged with awe.

"Zack?" Jack repeated.

CHAPTER SEVENTEEN

Cabo San Lucas, Baja California Sur

"You're late, Charles," Barbie remarked in a voice that reminded Charlie Diamond of the Good Witch in the old *Wizard of Oz* movie.

"If there's anything I hate more than parasites," she continued, "it's the lack of punctuality from my clients." She spoke without turning to look at Charlie, who'd entered the hermetically sealed upper room of the Pink Octopus. The air was chilled, and the black lighting cast an eerie glow to the sanitized walls.

"Sorry," Charlie said, his voice muffled by the filter mask that covered his nose and mouth. "I got tied up."

In addition to filtering his breath, Charlie was required to slip his shoes into sterilized paper slippers and wear surgical gloves. He shuffled across the room and sat heavily at a table made from carved Mayan stone tablets. He felt himself shiver and wondered if it was from the cold or the woman perched on the oversize circular dais in front of him. The platform was made from the blondest wood Charlie had ever seen, its surface waxed to a mirror finish.

Barbie stood on the oval stage surrounded by life-size dolls, her shaved head pulsing in the bluish light. She wore loose-fitting cotton undergarments and a starch-white bathrobe. One hand held a tube of lip gloss, the other a smokeless cigarette cartridge. Neither hand was gloved, and Charlie could see her nearly translucent nails extending past her long, pale fingers.

"Can you turn off the air-conditioning?" Charlie asked, crossing his arms for warmth.

The androgynous businesswoman ignored him as she dabbed at the lips of a half-dressed female mannequin. The life-size model had extra-large breasts tattooed to resemble the mouth of a margarita glass, each plastic nipple inked into a pointy wedge of lime. Tattooed beneath the breasts were glass stems running the length of the mannequin's belly where they abruptly plunged beneath a pair of neon pink panties.

Barbie stepped back and inspected her artwork. "She's my favorite, Charles. Have you seen her?"

"Las Margaritas," Charlie muttered as he peered around the silhouetted room. Dozens more anthropomorphic models populated the stage in a myriad of positions, their bodies glowing like jellyfish in the odd light. Some were clothed. Others were nude. All wore expressions and wigs that mimicked the topless women Charlie had seen dancing in the club. A few were placed in sexually provocative positions, and one bore a striking resemblance to the woman on the dais.

Charlie's attention returned to the center of the stage, where a gem-studded throne was flanked by two stone statues of Aztec gods. To the left was Coyolxauhqui, the moon goddess with her serpentine torso and prominent bosom. To the right was Coatlicue, mother of all gods, with her skeletal face framed by human hands. Both statues sat perched on pedestals. Charlie's eyes widened as he leaned across the table for a closer look.

"A recent purchase," Barbie said in her squeaky voice, her back still toward him. She turned and Charlie watched her place a plastic cigarette filter to her thin lips and puff.

"They must be worth a fortune," he said. "The quality is—"

"Museumesque?" she interrupted. "Indeed. You could say they are on permanent loan from a rather prominent exhibition in Mexico City."

"You had them stolen?"

Barbie puffed harder on the pseudo-cigarette and then said, "The reason for our visit." She reached out with her free hand and caressed the curls of a kneeling mannequin's long blonde wig. "As you no doubt are aware, Charles, the Jesuit Treasure has been unearthed."

Charlie cleared his throat and said nothing. He had begun to shiver uncontrollably.

Barbie dropped her hand from the wig and glared at Charlie, the slit that served as her mouth angling downward in disappointment.

"Um."

"Come now, Charles. Advertising is one thing, acting the fool is quite another. Maybe a hidden camera, say in a fish eye, would help with your performance."

Charlie reddened.

Barbie raised the plastic filter to her lips and drew a quick breath. "I have little birds everywhere, Charles. No secret escapes me." Her filterless hand floated down to the sallow shoulder of the mannequin. She feathered her fingers across the doll's waxen chest and paused at one of its two gravity-defying breasts. She plucked the nipple like a banjo string and took an extra-long drag on the electronic cigarette.

Charlie averted his eyes.

"Do you find my aversion to pathogens troubling?"

"Pathogens?"

"Microbes, Charlie. Dirty little organisms that breed and fester everywhere. Especially on warm hosts with cozy holes and crevices."

"When you put it like that."

Barbie strolled to her throne, and in a singsong tone said, "Did you know Ronald Stump is in La Paz? He'll be here tomorrow."

"At the club?"

Barbie wagged an alabaster finger through the air and sat. "Discreetness, Charles. Mr. Stump will be arriving in *Cabo* tomorrow. Where he goes after that is not your concern."

"Stump's an art collector," Charlie said, a hint of concern in his voice.

"A man with his resources knows many things."

"Are you offering it to him?"

"*It?*"

"The treasure."

"Ah, yes. Back to the treasure." She crossed her legs. "Possession of wealth is power, Charles. But like all possessions, such ownership is an evolving concept. Take the Pink Octopus as an example. I pay a great deal of money for the most beautiful dancers to entertain my clients. Special customers like you and possibly Mr. Stump. But who is it that I control? The women whom I pay handsomely or the clients I may one day extort?"

Charlie fidgeted.

"You seem reticent for a man whose billboard business I plan to double."

"You already know I was robbed last night," Charlie stuttered. "Two women set me up. They called my cell phone this morning and attempted to blackmail me."

Barbie's colorless eyes flashed knowingly.

"The maid was in on it. I'm sure of it. Find her and tell her I want my artwork back. The statues, too."

Barbie's hand flinched as though the electronic cigarette had become infused with static. "Are you threatening me, Charles?"

Charlie swallowed dryly. "Never."

"Then tell me, how many people have you told about the treasure?"

Charlie shrugged. "No one."

Barbie made a tsk-tsk sound with her tongue. "How long have *you* known?"

"I—" he noticed the sudden change in Barbie's eyes. "Last night," he stammered. "Before the…mishap. I had a message on my cell phone."

"And how much did Mr. Dixon say he wanted for it?"

"Twenty million."

Barbie took a long, slow pull on the plastic filter. "Are you a superstitious man, Charles?" she asked, exhaling invisible smoke into the air.

Charlie shook his head.

"Legend says that the treasure is cursed. A crown made from a sacred whale bone and studded with rare black pearls. A crown presented to the Jesuits by a local Indian chieftain. A nefarious gift to rid the land of the pious dogs who'd enslaved them mercilessly."

"Did it work?"

"You tell me. The Jesuits were banished, but it wasn't long before the Franciscans replaced them. And then the Dominicans. Some would say today's enslavers are the tourists and their mighty dollars."

"Are you saying the curse is real?"

"Isn't it? A priceless piece of art that promises not fortune, but ruin?"

"Nothing is priceless," he said, his voice suffused with a sudden longing.

"Charles," she said condescendingly. "Surely you cannot afford such a relic. Not after last night's…unfortunate affair."

"Goddamn you!"

Barbie sucked on the filter and narrowed her eyes with intrigue. "A distinct possibility. Now, how much would a man of your influence pay for this crown of pearls?"

Charlie took a deep breath. "Everything I have."

"And how much do you think Mr. Stump would pay for the privilege of cursing his enemies?"

The blood suddenly drained from Charlie's face.

"Nobody threatens me, Charlie. No one."

"I'm sorry," he whispered.

"A man of Mr. Stump's wealth can become rather treacherous when desirous of something so rare."

Charlie said nothing.

Barbie reached into the left-hand pocket of her robe and removed an antibacterial wipe. She wrapped the plastic filter and dropped it into the pocket.

"Those two women," she said, her voice far away. "The ones who stole your artwork."

"Yes."

"The evidence they possess of your *other* hobby could ruin you."

Charlie gave a nervous nod.

"If, by chance, I could broker a deal with them, I believe one million dollars would suffice to keep your secret safe and sound. Quite a bargain under the circumstances, yes?"

Charlie did not respond.

Barbie removed a paper filter mask from the right-hand pocket of her robe. "One million cash delivered here tomorrow night." She slipped the band of the mask over her bald head. "By you, personally," she added with a jab of her finger.

Before Charlie could respond, she pressed a button on the throne. A loud hissing noise filled the room as sprinklers affixed to the ceiling released clouds of antibacterial aerosol.

Charlie began coughing and raced from the room, laughter filling the air behind him.

CHAPTER EIGHTEEN

Punta Baja, Baja California Sur

After the second gunshot, Digby entered the cave and waited for another flash of lightning before retrieving the discarded gun. He spotted Zack curled into a protective ball and helped him outside and sat him down next to Jack, whose temple had ballooned like a lopsided squash. The rain was falling in great swaths filling the air with the scent of desert sage.

"What happened?" Jack asked his brother through half-swollen lips.

Zack didn't answer.

"Zack?"

"He can't hear you," Digby said, inspecting the deep claw marks along both sides of Zack's temples.

"Why not?"

"His ears are missing."

Jack looked sick. "You cut off his ears?"

"No. *Mapache grande* did."

"I thought you said the Indians were long gone."

Digby groaned impatiently. "Not *A*-pache. *Ma*-pache. Baja's giant raccoon. That was one of the biggest I've ever seen."

Jack began to shiver, less from the rain than from the thought of an enormous raccoon gnawing off his brother's ears.

Zack moaned. In the flashing light, his sideburns glistened red with blood. The rain began to fall harder.

Digby motioned with the gun and led the brothers back into the cave and out of the rain. He watched Jack lean close and inspect his brother's wounds.

"You better get him to a doctor," Digby said, pocketing the gun. He used his teeth to quickly loosen the knot at his wrists. The rope fell to the floor of the cave. "As soon as this rain stops. His scalp looks like Swiss cheese."

"I can barely see," Jack protested. "My head's on fire and I feel dizzy. No way I can drive out of here."

"Not my problem."

"You can't just leave us here," Jack said and lunged.

Digby rolled toward the twin's blind side. Jack flailed at the air and collapsed to the dirt.

Digby aimed the barrel of the pistol. "Try that again and I swear to God I'll shoot you."

"Please don't leave us here," Jack blubbered, his working eye beginning to leak tears.

"The best you're going to get," Digby said through gritted teeth, "is me following you out of the mountains once the rain lets up. When we hit pavement, you and your brother are heading east to Santa Rosalia. Thirty minutes, tops, to the hospital. As far as I'm concerned we never met."

Jack slumped to the ground, whimpering.

Two hours later the sky cleared and Digby stepped toward the brightness of the cave entrance. He held the pistol ready and waved for the twins to join him. Both were shivering with fever.

"Let's go."

The two men crawled into a shaft of sunlight where Digby stood shading his eyes from the afternoon sun.

"I'll be goddamned," he said, removing his hat and glancing toward the arroyo where both trucks had been parked.

Jack strained his good eye. "Someone stole the trucks."

Digby wagged the gun at the crashing waves. "Yours is in the surf. Mine's stuck halfway down the wash."

Jack tapped his brother on the shoulder and pointed. Their old Toyota was upside down, the bald tires washed clean by the crashing waves. Digby's full-size F-150 stood upright, its axles buried in wet sand, the cab wedged between a boulder and the trunk of a large mesquite tree. A tangle of twisting branches wrapped the bow of the aluminum skiff in a thorny hug.

"Change of plan," he said, and started toward the arroyo. "See you around."

"You leave us here and we'll die," Jack protested. "Zack's got kids. Little ones."

Digby stopped. "Zack's a father?"

"Two girls and a boy. Back in Tucson." He sighed. "We weren't going to hurt you. I swear. We ain't killers. We never done nothing like this before. Zack's a part-time custodian at the college. I got disability. When this job came along we jumped at it. You got to believe me, mister."

Digby was silent.

"Take Zack with you," Jack went on. "Drop him at the hospital. I'll be okay. Ain't nobody gonna miss me when I'm gone."

Digby pocketed the gun, and then combed a hand through tangles of damp hair. "You could have killed me in the mountains." He glanced down at the aluminum skiff caught in the tree. "It's too damn risky hauling those artifacts out by boat. One wave and it's gone forever." He stared hard at Jack. "You help me hide it up here in the cave, and I'll take you both with me."

Jack tried to smile, but instead flinched with pain. "Okay."

"I don't like the look of the wind, but if we're lucky we'll make it by dark."

"Make it where?"

"The marina at Santa Rosalia. From there it's about a mile walk to the hospital on the hill." He started down the path, hoping he could buy a used truck and get back to the arroyo before the twins had a change of heart.

"Hey mister!" Jack called out.

Digby stopped and turned.

"Sorry we kidnapped you."

Digby eyed the falling sun and said, "We need to hurry. See if you can find your brother's ears. If they aren't chewed up, maybe the doctor can sew them back on."

CHAPTER NINETEEN

La Paz, Baja California Sur

Fish splashed down on Bahía de La Paz and taxied his seaplane toward the old ferry dock, where a 200-foot mega-yacht glimmered above the waterline. It was midafternoon, and a pair of mahogany-skinned women lounged topless beside a diamond-shaped swimming pool.

Above the pool deck was a third tier with a small helicopter and an emerald-colored cigarette boat. And above that, offset behind an angled wall of tinted glass, sat the helm, brimming with electronics.

Fish raised a pair of binoculars and read the fancy gold letters stenciled across both sides of the bow: STUMP.

He slid open the plane's side window and filled his lungs with fresh air. Through the sound system came Tom Waits singing about bloody fingers on a purple knife.

Fish smiled. "Showtime."

He threaded the plane through a smattering of sailboats listing with the falling tide, and stomped hard on the left rudder to avoid a sunken ketch whose mossy green mast hung thick with guano. A flock of pelicans squawked at the intrusion and lifted clumsily into the air.

Moments later the seaplane slowed at the side of the large cement dock. Fish spun the plane sideways and shut down the twin engines. He unclipped his harness and watched a young Mexican boy appear with a dock line that he used to secure the starboard float to a cleat.

Fish unlatched the cargo door, hefted a large canvas bag over his shoulder, and freed Mephistopheles from his paddock at the rear of the plane. He slid open the door and swung his leg over the bare back of Mephistopheles. The mule neighed in response, stepped to the dock, and shook out her patterned mane. Fish reached into the pocket of his sailcloth pants and held out a hundred-peso note. The boy accepted the tip with a wide grin.

"*Cuida el aeroplano?*" Fish asked kindly, and then nudged Mephistopheles toward the gangway of the idling mega-yacht.

A fit young man in a gold-trimmed sailor outfit stood guard at the top of the gangway. Fish acknowledged the man with a touch to the brim of his mullet-skin cap, gently kicked the mule, and rode onto the boat. The man jumped back with a start.

"Stump knows I'm coming," Fish called out.

Mephistopheles rounded the back deck and rode up the short stairway to the salon where two men sat beneath a veranda at an oval glass table playing chess. The board was made of turquoise and the pieces were fashioned from onyx and ivory.

Fish lifted the bill of his cap and looked down at the odd pair. He recognized the older man's sneer and badly disguised toupee. The real estate mogul wore a fitted suit, exotic leather shoes, and a gem-encrusted Rolex refracting the afternoon sunlight like a kaleidoscope.

The man beside him was tall and thin with tightly corded muscles wrapping his arms like jungle vines. A tattooed rattlesnake coiled down each bicep and forearm, ending in a set of bloody fangs inked across the man's knuckles.

One of the thin man's eyes was covered in a patch, the other staring unblinkingly, its pupil small and black as pitch. His face could have been carved from quartz, and he wore a black muscle shirt and tight jeans. Clearly visible at the crown of a tightly cropped head was the image of Christ tattooed on a cross, the sacred blood trickling down the sides of the man's elongated neck.

A tattoo that stirred something just shy of a memory in Fish, as did the man's face. Fish's gaze was taking in the combat knives strapped to the man's triceps, and the hunting knife hanging from his waistband, when the man started to rise.

But the real estate mogul waved him off. Fish trotted Mephistopheles to the edge of the glass table and stopped.

"Gentlemen," he said with a tip of his hat.

"If I didn't know any better," Ronald Stump commented, "I'd say Crocodile Dundee just rode aboard my yacht."

The rattlesnakes pulsed as the bodyguard chuckled.

Ronald Stump's eyes lowered to the mule. "Perhaps you could remove your livestock to the dock."

"Mephistopheles has a thing for overpriced boats." Fish reached out and patted the mule on her flank, surreptitiously loosening the machete sheathed tightly to his thigh.

"Mephistopheles?"

"Appaloosa half-breed." Fish swung down from the mule's back and landed softly on bare feet. He unslung the canvas bag from his shoulder and let it drop to the plush gold carpeting.

The thin man's left hand reached toward a knife. Stump waved him off for the second time in as many minutes.

"Are you a pro wrestling fan?" Stump asked Fish.

"Not so much."

"Shame." He motioned a manicured finger toward his bodyguard. "Meet Snake Hissken. Two-time WWF champion."

"That explains the eye patch."

The bodyguard's nostrils flared.

"Something to drink, Mr. Fish?" Stump asked, snapping his fingers. A thirty-something woman appeared wearing a string bikini. Her eyes were hidden behind mirrored sunglasses and her upper torso shimmered with suntan oil. She slowly refilled their cocktail glasses.

"No thanks," Fish said and watched the woman walk confidently back to her sunshine. Fish turned to Stump. "This isn't

Cabo. Your waitress and the topless party by the pool should wear more clothes while in port."

"Noted," Stump said without concern.

"Prick," Snake remarked.

Fish brushed a hand down his braided goatee and let his fingers linger on the metal fisherman's crimp.

Stump said, "You mentioned Mr. Hissken's eye patch."

"I seem to remember Kurt Russell wearing one just like it."

Stump shook his head. "I can assure you the eye patch is no Hollywood affectation."

The bodyguard raised the eye patch and revealed an empty socket.

"My condolences," Fish said.

The afternoon sun slipped beneath the awning and reflected sharply off the chessboard. Stump pressed a button on the arm of his chair. The mechanized awning dropped six inches and a series of small nozzles appeared along the edge of the canvas frill, sending a cooling mist across the deck. Mephistopheles twitched her ears at the sudden change in temperature.

Stump sipped his cocktail and said, "Your associate back in Arizona, Ms. Toozie McGill. She was rather insistent we meet in person."

"Smart woman."

"She said you live here permanently. That you rarely travel north." He took a sip of icy booze. "Sounds like you're hiding from something, Mr. Fish."

"I consider Baja paradise. I see no reason to leave."

"Surely you miss the conveniences. Pleasantries only money can buy. Five-star restaurants, entertainment, a world-class marina?"

"Nope."

Stump's poker face showed no reaction, and for a long beat he held Fish's stare. Then the real estate baron's eyes softened and he said, "Lucky for you I was on my way to Cabo when Ms. McGill called."

"Somehow I don't feel so lucky."

The tattooed blood of Christ pulsed down Snake's carotid artery, and Fish sensed the man would gladly gut him like a flounder if given the chance.

Stump said, "You rode a mule onto my boat without consequence. I'd call that lucky." He turned to Snake. "Wouldn't you agree, Mr. Hissken?"

"Don't believe in luck," the bodyguard scoffed, fingering the Christ inked into his scalp. "The Lord works in mysterious ways."

"I'll keep that in mind," Fish commented.

Snake's brow twisted into a knot. "You look familiar. Shorter hair, no goatee, and maybe I've seen you on TV."

"Doubtful," Fish lied, and turned his attention to Stump, who was starting to look bored. "You mentioned disrespect. You tried to buy Espíritu Santo recently in order to turn it into a private fantasy island. Did you really think you could build a gated community with casinos and golf courses on one of Baja's most spectacular islands?"

Stump glared.

"The amount of damage you'd have done to the environment," Fish continued, "would have been irreversible. Dredging for marinas, fertilizer runoff for the lawns and fairways. Do you know that the waters around there are home to one of the world's few whale shark rookeries? That from the north end you can kayak to the famous seamount where Jacques Cousteau filmed the circling hammerhead sharks?"

Snake stood with surprising speed, the hunting knife gripped in his outstretched hand.

Stump smiled. "The man can say what he wants, Snake. He's got an island to sell. He's just airing regret at a wasted life."

Snake lowered the knife. He quickly crossed himself—such a devout fellow, Fish thought with uncomfortable familiarity—but remained standing.

Fish locked his eyes again on Stump. "You think because I'm an American you can appeal to my Yankee greed? Turn Mag Bay into a rich man's wet dream?"

The skin beneath Stump's right eye twitched. "Ms. McGill said you were interested in selling."

"To the Nature Conservancy maybe. But to some soulless real estate developer? Never."

"What's your price?" Stump asked with a sneer.

Fish kicked the canvas bag toward the table. "This is a million in cash. To keep your development plans the hell out of Magdalena Bay." He reached into the back pocket of his sailcloth pants and removed a folded set of papers. "Sign here, and Mephistopheles and I will be on our way."

Snake turned to Stump, who nodded. The bodyguard retrieved the bag from the carpet, and then reached for the contract. "A time to kill and a time to heal," he hissed the biblical verse into Fish's ear.

Fish gave no response. The man snatched the contract from Fish's hand and returned to the glass table. He handed the document to Stump, and then slowly spilled the bundles of cash across the glass top.

Stump scanned the documents.

Fish yawned.

Mephistopheles raised her tail and fertilized the carpet.

"Fucking donkey!" Snake yelled, and lunged with his knife.

The blade sliced into the animal's spotted mane just as the hilt of Fish's machete crushed the bodyguard's temple. Snake crumpled to the ground, the knife bouncing harmlessly across the carpet.

"She's a mule," Fish said, and sheathed the machete. He strode to the table. "Mag Bay's off-limits. Sign the contract and you'll never see me again."

"And if I refuse?"

"Hire more bodyguards."

Stump eyed the unconscious man. "He's going to kill you for that."

"I wouldn't bet on it."

The real estate mogul shrugged, and then scribbled his signature on the document. "Good luck enforcing this in a Mexican court."

"I'll do my own enforcing," Fish said, tucking the agreement into his waistband and pulling himself astride Mephistopheles. "You just got something for nothing, Mr. Stump. I wouldn't look a gift mule in the mouth if I were you."

He tipped his fish-skin cap and rode down the gangway and out to his waiting seaplane.

CHAPTER TWENTY

El Rosario, Baja California Sur

Slim Dixon drove his convertible Cadillac up and down the dirt streets of El Rosario until he spotted the shiny black Silverado with the Dually tires and dented front bumper. It was backed tightly into the graveled driveway of a small adobe house enclosed by a chain-link fence. The front yard was raked dirt, and the side yards surrounded by mesquite and Palo Verde trees. Towering bougainvilleas shrouded the porch, where a lone rocking chair rested beside a rustic handmade table. Slim passed the house and parked.

The midafternoon heat shimmied in an oily mirage down the corrugated tin roof, and even the sky seemed to fade from blue to white hot. No other cars were parked along the dirt road, and aside from Slim no other person seemed interested in confronting the harsh afternoon.

The hit man felt a raging in his head as he belted the stag knife to his waist. He loaded the pistol and screwed on the silencer, walked quietly to the low gate, and let himself into the yard.

Killing a man for damaging the Cadillac was overzealous, he knew. But the driver hadn't stopped to offer assistance or payment or even to apologize. Instead, the man just cranked up the music and continued on his way as if Slim and his classic car were nothing more than horsefeathers on the side of the road. It was more than a taunt. It was a thrown gauntlet, the first blow of an unfinished fight. A fight that Slim planned to end quickly.

As the hit man approached the house, he watched the front door slowly open behind a torn screen. His hand went to the pistol tucked behind his back.

An elderly woman in a bright shawl stepped onto the porch. She carried a crying baby in her arms. Somewhere in the house an argument flared. A young woman's voice rising in rapid Spanish. Short, clipped baritone responses. Slim imagined the young cowboy and his girlfriend arguing about the accident. About the damage to the truck's front bumper. About the gringo going to the cops. Slim snickered to himself. A kid with a truck like that probably owned the local cops.

He watched the old woman sit in the rocking chair, her sole concentration on the child in her lap. A glass shattered, and he heard the old woman begin a lullaby in Spanish. Slim backed away from the gate unseen. He walked briskly to the truck in the driveway, glad to have the bank of bougainvilleas blocking the view from the porch. He checked the silencer and emptied six bullets, one into each tire, and felt the edge of his anger dull slightly.

He tucked the gun into his belt and freed the stag knife from its sheath. Then he opened the passenger door and slit the leather seat from end to end. He slashed the dashboard and punctured the side paneling until it was pulp. The rage was fading, replaced by a new hunger. Real and insatiable.

Lobster burritos and cold cervezas held his attention now. Before a much-deserved afternoon siesta to refresh the body and mind before continuing south. Besides, splattering the stranger's brains across the old woman's bougainvilleas would only invite further distractions.

Slim sheathed the blade, pleased with his pragmatism. He had a long night of driving ahead. But unlike most Baja visitors, Slim was looking forward to the dangers of the two-lane gauntlet of shoulderless asphalt. The swerving big rigs, desultory cattle, and cavernous potholes were small payment for the joy that awaited him: the payoff that added a sudden spryness to his step.

Blood *and* riches.

What could be better than that?

CHAPTER TWENTY-ONE

Sea of Cortez, Baja California Sur

One-eyed Jack sat hunched at the skiff's bow, his swollen face shielded by an arm blocking the waves ricocheting off the hull. His twin brother, Zack, lay in a ball at his feet, moaning in pain each time the spray of saltwater soaked his earless head. Digby drove, his wide-brimmed hat tight to his brow, fighting to ignore a mounting dread. They'd left Punta Baja an hour earlier on a mostly calm sea. Now the wind was driving at twenty-five knots and gusting at more than thirty.

"Halfway there!" Digby shouted into the cresting waves. The archaeologist was crouched at the stern maneuvering the outboard through the rising sea. At the top of each wave, he could see a vista of water kicking and bucking as if currents of electricity flowed beneath. To his right, the shoreline faded in a salty mist.

Digby was regretting the decision to regroup in Santa Rosalia when he spotted a sailboat scudding gracefully in the distance. He angled toward it, gunning the engine up another steep wave. The skiff cascaded over a lip of boiling water and dropped into the adjoining trough with a hull-shuddering thud.

"Can you slow down?" Jack cried out. "I think Zack's going to pass out."

"We'll get swamped."

They had just porpoised over another wave when the engine sputtered and died. Digby hauled back on the starter cord. Nothing. He yanked out the choke and tried again. Silence. He opened the throttle and rhythmically worked the cord, but the engine refused to fire. The waves spun the skiff sideways, teetering it violently from gunwale to gunwale.

"Hope you two can swim," Digby said.

"What?" Jack asked, his face ashen.

"Swim! Can you swim?" Digby repeated, making freestyle motions with his arms. His hat slipped free and Frisbeed across the whitecaps.

"I'm afraid of sharks."

Jack was also afraid of losing his brother's ear. He'd found only one in the cave, torn cleanly off at its root. He'd shoved it into his pocket along with the gold coin he'd taken from the trunk before catching the ill-fated stingray. Before, their grand plan was shanghaied by a rabid raccoon. Now, as the boat pitched and stalled, Jack jammed his hand into his pocket and gripped the two similarly sized objects. One firm and promising, the other pliant and misshapen.

"The sharks have been fished out," Digby yelled, reassuringly, just before a towering wave cartwheeled the skiff and flung all three passengers into the sea.

The boat rolled over and the weight of the outboard engine began to sink the stern. Digby plunged beneath the surface. He unhinged the motor, loosening the clamps between breaths of air, mindful not to rake himself across the propeller. On the third dive, the clamps released and the engine sank into the fathoms. The skiff's Styrofoam insulation bobbed it to the surface like a sunning turtle.

As it moved with the current, Digby fought through a cresting wave and gripped the ridgelike chines running the length of the hull and searched the white water for signs of the twins. He squinted through the salty spray when an earless head appeared above the waves. As the swell passed, he could see Zack, holding his one-eyed brother in a lifeguard grip, swimming one-handed toward the boat.

"Where'd you learn that?" Digby asked, momentarily forgetting the kidnapper's loss of hearing.

Zack pushed his brother to the hull next to Digby.

Jack coughed out a mouthful of water and said, "Zack competed in high school."

"I thought twins did everything together."

"Me, I play accordion."

Before Digby could respond, Zack hauled himself out of the water and sat at the peak of the hull, clamping his knees to the keel like a bull rider. He waved his arms frantically until a powerful gust threw him into a hunchbacked wave. He quickly remounted the hull and waved again.

"What the hell's he doing?" Jack panted, the color slowly returning to his swollen face.

"Saving our lives," Digby answered.

Ten minutes later, a forty-eight-foot schooner with a smiling Medusa maidenhead rising from the bow slashed through the swells and then turned hard to port, falling off the wind fifty yards away. A young woman in baggy sweats and a tie-dyed long-sleeved T-shirt hailed from the helm. As the current brought the boat closer, Digby could see colorful whales breaching across her chest. Her red hair hung in a loose ponytail beneath a yellow bandana. She checked the telltale at the top of the mast, and then pitched a life ring into the waves, the length of nylon rope following like a sea serpent.

As the circle of bright-orange foam floated within range, Zack wrapped an arm around Jack's chest and swam away from the skiff. He helped his brother grip the life ring and gave an okay sign. The sailor hauled Jack across the water. Zack quickly returned to the skiff and motioned for Digby.

"You first," Digby said.

Zack pointed at his missing ears and shrugged.

Digby jabbed a finger at the twin. "Go!"

Zack shook his head and redoubled his grip on the hull. Digby had grabbed him harshly when a trilling whistle caused him to look up. The schooner had angled closer and the sailor was standing at the bow, a stern look on her face.

"I don't know what the hell you two are doing," she called out, "but this is a rescue. The man on board is injured and the wind's not dying down. Now get your asses on board!"

Digby tapped Zack on the back and pointed toward the sailboat. "Together," he said and motioned with his arms.

Moments later the two men climbed aboard the schooner.

"For fuck's sake," the sailor said, wrapping a towel around Zack's shivering shoulders. "This guy's in worse shape than the other one." She looked at Digby. "What the hell happened out there?"

"Long story," Digby said, his voice suddenly tremulous with fatigue. He noticed the Tibetan symbols tattooed across the tops of the woman's bare feet, and the way she moved in sync with the sway of the boat. "Thank you," he quickly added.

"Molly," the sailor said, extending her hand. "Towels are in the deck box, starboard side."

Digby walked to the starboard gunwale and removed two dry towels. He returned and handed one to Molly. Then he stripped from his wet shirt and wrapped the remaining towel around his chest.

"Duncan Rigby," he offered. "Digby. I'm an archaeologist from the University of Arizona." He combed nervously at his mustache with a free hand, glancing around the expansive teakwood deck. "Beautiful boat," he said, turning to face her.

Molly eyed the shark tooth tattoo.

"Megalodon," Digby explained before she could ask. "The ocean's largest predator, once upon a time. Probably the world's. Found it while digging in the mountains above Todos Santos."

Molly barely registered an acknowledgment. "Those two need a doctor," she said motioning toward the mast where the twins huddled for warmth. "Closest one I know of is Santa Rosalia. I'll drop you off at the marina."

"I'm not with them," Digby said.

Molly narrowed her gaze.

"I mean, I am and I'm not."

"Listen, Duncan. Or Rigby or whatever your name is. I don't like the look of this. I may be a lone sailor, but I'm not some lass in need of a knight. So quit the bullshit. At this point the marina's the best you're going to get."

Digby felt for the gold coins for the used truck he planned to buy in Santa Rosalia. They had fallen out during his underwater plunge. "I'll give you an IOU to take me back to Punta Baja."

"Not interested."

"But my skiff…" Digby said, and glanced back at the skiff, half-sunk in the distance. When he turned back, he was staring at a loaded speargun.

"Who the hell are you and what exactly happened to these men?"

Digby stumbled backward, palms held outward. He blinked, thinking fast. Too many things had gone wrong since finding the treasure. It was time to take a chance.

"Ever heard of the Jesuit Treasure?"

CHAPTER TWENTY-TWO

Tucson, Arizona

It was midafternoon by the time Toozie McGill pulled her old diesel pickup into the parking lot of the Arizona State Museum. Earlier that morning she'd talked with Atticus Fish and informed him of the last-minute meeting in La Paz with real estate mogul Ronald Stump. Asked him to fly over the dirt roads leading into the canyons of the Tres Virgenes mountain range. Fly a few grid patterns in search of the missing archaeologist's truck.

Atticus had been eager to help. He'd also invited her to his island for an open-ended getaway. The handsome attorney even buttressed the invitation with offers to explore rarely visited beaches, fish for elusive black snook, and feast on world-famous sand dab tostadas at his seaside bar. Not once had he mentioned the issue of his ex-wife, Elizabeth, the woman Toozie's father had affectionately called Onezie.

It had been ten years since Toozie's older sister had died. Ten years since her brother-in-law, Francis Finch, took one of life's curveballs on the chin. The result was a boatload of booze and a brilliant legal theory that would veer him so far from the edge of normalcy that Toozie was certain he wouldn't survive. But survive he did. And with an extraordinary measure of élan.

Widowed at the age of thirty, childless and alone, Francis Finch sobered up long enough to file the most infamous class-action lawsuit in history: a multifaceted complaint against organized religion. An assault against God is what some called it, with the tabloids quickly labeling him "Lawyer Lucifer" and "Billionaire Beelzebub."

In actuality, the court filings were a wondrous waltz of legal maneuvering that targeted a well-known insurance company for refusing to pay a life insurance claim after lightning struck and killed one of its policyholders. The claim was denied under a catch-all exclusion known as the "Acts of God" clause that protected insurance companies against loss whenever Mother Nature went on a rampage. Earthquakes, tsunamis, volcanic eruptions, and the like.

Sure, a policyholder could pay for the specialized coverage, but the fees were astronomical, and other than a few wealthy customers, no one ever did. Including Bishop Douglas McFetters. The bishop, Finch's good friend, was conducting a wedding ceremony in Flagstaff, Arizona, in a meadow surrounded by a grove of pines. Towering green lightning rods that burst into flames when a powerful bolt descended from the heavens. The bishop was killed instantly, and because the good father had no specific lightning coverage, the insurance company blamed the death on an act of God. The bishop's sister appealed the ruling, and wrote a letter as beneficiary of her brother's million-dollar policy. The response from the claims department was swift and short:

CLAIM DENIED.

So the sister went to Francis Finch, who was incensed enough to file suit. He deposed dozens of executives at the life insurance company and discovered a startling, if somewhat esoteric, fact: regardless of their individual religions, every insurance company executive defended the Acts of God exclusion through the teachings of their individual faiths. The Christians welcomed the exclusion, as did the handful of Jews and the one Muslim manager. In fact, the two Catholic senior vice presidents even claimed that the heads of their churches endorsed the fact that "Mother Nature" was but a pseudonym for God.

Intrigued, Finch widened his net and subpoenaed the priests, rabbis, and imams. The result was a blockade in the form of high-priced defense attorneys filing cease-and-desist orders. The judge agreed and placed everything on hold while she considered the evidence. Which was code for dismissal of the lawsuit. So Finch got wily. He went public. Local television, late-night cable, radio, print. Every media outlet that wanted an interview with the legal version of the Prince of Darkness got one.

The result was a plethora of phone calls from potential clients whose loved ones had been killed by rockslides or wind shears, or in one case a rogue wave while sunbathing at a nude beach in Northern California. Finch agreed to represent them all. He also grew curious about the pervasiveness of the Acts of God–based denials. He placed ads in national newspapers and popular magazines, and soon had so many clients that the judge reluctantly agreed to class-action status. She also released her hold on the subpoenas and agreed to allow Finch to depose the religious leaders. Which he did with renewed vim and a refocused strategy. He completely ignored the insurance companies, and instead honed in on the bishops, the pastors, the Talmudists, the maharajas, the televangelists, and anyone else who claimed to channel the word of God. The strategy was simple: uncover the link between life insurance and the existence of God and force a settlement for his clients. Expose the theological endorsements of the Acts of God exclusion, and shame the companies to pay up.

No more fine print.

Dead was dead.

And so Finch confronted his adversaries with benign questions about the Almighty. Was He really omnipotent, omniscient, omnibenevolent? Were the sunrise, the sunset, the sea breeze, the sunshine all godly blessings? If so, what about volcanoes and hurricanes and lightning storms?

Then, once he'd established the connection between God and Mother Nature, Finch quoted directly from the various insurance policies, reading the Acts of God exclusion word for word. Next, he asked the religious leaders if insurance companies were correct in claiming that God caused the lightning to strike Bishop McFetters, and he demanded to know if God caused the killer tsunamis, the deadly typhoons, the suffocating rogue waves.

Of course, Finch knew the answers before he asked the questions. Knew that no one could give him a definitive yes. The lawyer had the worshippers boxed in, which in effect boxed in the insurance companies: without agreement from God's representatives that God caused the deaths of their claimants, the insurance companies' denials lacked credibility.

In other words, there was no official endorsement to buttress the denials. No legal proof that God had caused any of the deaths. The insurance companies were relying on a generalized deference to an omnipotent God in order to deny tens of thousands of annual claims worldwide. The profit savings were in the billions of dollars, and all of it at the expense of dead policyholders and their grieving beneficiaries.

Still, the insurance companies refused to settle. And so Finch unleashed a hoard of accountants to pry into their charitable donation history. He demanded to know how much money insurance companies added to the divine coffers of religious institutions. To prove a financial connection between the Almighty and Allstate, Yahweh and MetLife, the Lord and Lloyd's of London.

He demanded to know how many of the billions of dollars in religious donations worldwide were the result of insurance company philanthropy. The defense lawyers screamed irrelevance. Finch countered that any form of doctrinal lobbying was far from irrelevant. The judge allowed the line of questioning, but warned Finch that the information might not be permissible as evidence at trial. Finch immediately petitioned all financial records, as well as the names of every accountant employed by the various religious institutions over the past several decades.

It was a bluff. Finch knew the judge would be reluctant to allow church records into court. Not unless Finch had actual proof of collusion between insurance company denials and religious institution hierarchy. He didn't. His only evidence was circumstantial: insurance companies needed organized religion to tacitly ordain their Act of God exclusion. And while religion didn't explicitly participate in insurance company decisions, the holy men were pleased to benefit by the relationship. So Fish played his ace in the hole. He anonymously informed the media of the scandalous—albeit loose—connection between insurance company denials and religious donations.

The timing proved cosmic. Church sex scandals were on the rise, and no competing religion wanted in on the correlation. And so, in a remarkable flash of cooperation, all of God's representatives agreed to end the lawsuit and help the insurance companies settle quickly and quietly. Anything to bury a potential new scandal and get back to doing what they did best: marketing divinity.

An offer was quickly proffered: one day of donations worldwide. From every denomination represented. The total was billions of dollars. It was the largest class-action settlement in history, and the 40 percent attorney fee enriched Francis Finch to aristocratic status. It also unleashed the fanatics. Unlike Salman Rushdie, who'd angered a single religion, Francis Finch had angered them all.

His fee of nearly a billion dollars sent the extremists into a tailspin, and so the lawyer fled south-of-the-border in search of solitude and safety. He burned his courtroom clothes, grew his hair and goatee, bought an island and a mule, and changed his name. Francis Finch the infamous class-action attorney became Atticus Fish the expatriated, eccentric American bar owner.

Ten years had passed, and yet Toozie felt her heart race at the thought of seeing the dashing man again. Feelings she had suppressed during those difficult weeks and months after her sister's passing. Feelings she'd all but forgotten in the years since. Until recently, when the charismatic lawyer with the square jaw and sea-green eyes had resurfaced and called requesting her help.

His boat, the eighty-two-foot *Wahoo Rhapsody*, had been stolen and its captain and crew tortured by an elusive drug lord. Toozie agreed to take the case, and they'd seen each other briefly at Catalina Island. After Fish agreed to meet the drug lord and exchange a million dollars in cash for the safety of his friends and their boat. He'd asked her out then, too. And she'd agreed. But a private investigator's travel plans have a way of unraveling. Workloads shift like monsoon winds. But now she was immersed in a potential kidnapping in Fish's beloved new country. In his veritable backyard of Baja California.

Was it fate or something else? she wondered as she shut down the engine of her truck. Or could it be simple coincidence that the archaeologist disappeared within flying distance of her ex-brother-in-law's sand dune island?

She hoped it was the former as she stepped onto the museum's broiling pavement and felt the heat waves radiate through the soles of her hand-stitched boots. It was early June, and the Tucson summer was already in full desert meltdown.

She brushed a lock of elderberry hair from her face and started walking.

CHAPTER TWENTY-THREE

Sea of Cortez, Baja California Sur

Standing on the back deck of the *Taliswoman* with his hands raised, Digby explained what he'd meant by the Jesuit Treasure. Molly slowly lowered the speargun. "Lucky for you I've read about the treasure. Never really believed it." She adjusted the mainsail and moved to the open wheelhouse. "Tell me more," she said and steered a course for Santa Rosalia.

Digby gave Molly a brief history of the Spanish conquest of Baja California. How the Jesuits were officially sent to convert the natives to Christianity, while secretly searching for the famed lost city of gold. A city popularized by Montalvo's novel, *The Adventures of Esplandián*, written in early 1500. In it, a mythical island called California was ruled by Queen Calafia and her tribe of beautiful Amazonian women who battled their enemies with weapons of gold.

At first, Baja California seemed a likely candidate for this island paradise. Until the priests landed on the desolate shoreline and discovered its dearth of female warriors and complete lack of gold weaponry. This supposed island of gold was so inhospitable that most of the padres requested leave almost immediately. A few, however, saw an opportunity to enslave local Indians and build a workforce of miners.

Placer mines were soon developed, and over the years the wily priests accumulated caches of silver and gold. The ore was smelted, fashioned into churchly artifacts, and supplemented with magnificent pearls culled from the waters off La Paz. And all of it was done without informing the king of Spain who, upon discovering the betrayal, ordered the priests expelled. Demanded they be brought back to Spain with their valuable treasure.

The priests, however, had loyal spies in the homeland who sent word of the king's order months before the soldiers arrived. The Jesuits hastily collected their wealth, reserving a few choice pieces for the king, before burying the remainder in the remote canyon high up in the Tres Virgenes mountain range. A single map was kept secret in anticipation of their return. But then the years turned to centuries, and eventually only rumors of the treasure remained. And whispers of a map. All without proof.

"Until now," Digby finished.

"And you just happened upon this one and only map," Molly asked skeptically. She heeled expertly into the late afternoon wind, yawing occasionally into the quartering sea.

"Yes," Digby answered sincerely, and described the day in the museum archives, the false floor of the old trunk, and the harried trip south. He explained finding the massive vein of crisscrossing quartz, the unearthing of the treasure, and his abduction by the twins. Then he told her of the mishap with the stingray and the encounter with *mapache grande*.

"Okay," she said. "Nobody makes up a tale like that."

She set the boat's autopilot for the Santa Rosalia marina, and then turned her attention to the two passengers huddled against the mast. She removed a fresh towel from the deck box and draped it over their waists. "At ten knots we'll be dockside in little over and hour."

She glanced up at the sky, and then tightened the mizzen stays. She quickly checked the shrouds and cleats, and reset a worn baggywrinkle where one of the mainsails was chafing against its standing rigging.

"We'll drop these two at the dock and head straight back to Punta Baja. I'd like to see this infamous treasure."

Digby's face softened in the afternoon sunlight. "I appreciate it."

CHAPTER TWENTY-FOUR

Tucson, Arizona

Toozie hurried from the heat and into the red brick building and within minutes was sitting in an air-conditioned foyer awaiting the arrival of Stanley Cohen, the Arizona State Museum's curator. Behind the counter, a dark-haired graduate student snapped chewing gum and rifled through a *National Geographic* magazine. At the sound of the curator's footsteps she said "Voilà!" without looking up. "The man himself!"

Toozie stood. She was especially tall in her rugged cowboy boots, and her recently dyed hair was loosely braided and dropped well past her shoulder blades. She wore no makeup, but her opalescent eyes and silver earrings highlighted a face as understated as it was luminous. She awaited the approaching footfalls, and watched a slight man with a balding head and wire-rimmed glasses enter the lobby.

"Ms. McGill," he said, his New York accent out of place in the cacti-studded Southwest.

"It's a pleasure to meet you, Mr. Cohen." Toozie shook his hand. "Sounds like you've spent some time in New York."

"Grew up in Soho."

"Nice."

The museum curator motioned down the hallway. "Please," he said and walked back toward his office.

Toozie followed him to a tidy room with floor-to-ceiling bookshelves lining the walls. Art books, mostly. And cookbooks. Rows of cookbooks.

"The art books are no surprise," Toozie said pleasantly, "but cookbooks? How do you have the time?"

Stanley paused behind his desk. He removed his glasses and cleaned the lenses with a mauve handkerchief he kept tucked in his shirt pocket. When he sat, he carefully folded the cloth and slipped it back into place.

He peered at her through sparkling lenses. "I'm strictly nine-to-five these days," he said coolly. "Plenty of time for a hobby."

"I thought half a curator's job was to fund-raise. Wining and dining at fancy restaurants every night. The big expense account. A perk, I suppose, if you like that sort of thing."

"Fancy restaurants? Here, in Tucson? Are you mad?"

Toozie brightened at the aspersion. "I've been called worse."

"A figure of speech. Forgive me if it offended you."

"Not at all." She leaned forward. "Have you tried Michelangelo's? It's not as well known as Vivace's or Café Poca Cosa, but it's quite a restaurant."

Stanley leaned back in his leather chair, his eyes distant. "Four years of prep school, a master's in fine art from NYU, and a PhD in classical studies from Yale. You'd think a pedigree like that, along with my specialty in coins and rare metals, would place me at the Met. Or at worst, the Museum of Fine Arts in Boston. I'm no gentile. We've had enough of these godforsaken deserts."

"Hallelujah for air-conditioning."

Stanley didn't smile. "The Southwest's a wasteland when it comes to the arts. They make a good show of it, but it's nothing compared to what we have back east."

"Then why take the job?"

"They offered me head curator straight out of school. That plus a hell of a salary. Seemed too good to pass up at the time. I've been regretting it since the day I set foot here."

"When was that?"

"1980."

Toozie whistled. "Sounds like curator positions don't open too often."

"Not the one I want."

"The Met?"

"The Smithsonian."

"You've been waiting thirty years for a job at the Smithsonian?"

"Not just any job. Curator of Mexican American art at the American History Museum."

"Mexican American? I'd have guessed something more European."

"Yes, well…"

Toozie noticed his right hand go to the ancient jade bracelet on his left wrist. He was no longer looking at her, focusing instead on the yellow blossoms of a Palo Verde tree growing just beyond his office window. His focus slowly returned and he said, "But we aren't here to talk about my career choices, now, are we?"

"I guess not," Toozie said. "Thank you for meeting with me on such short notice. Duncan Rigby's sister is worried about her brother. She thinks he might be in some kind of trouble."

"Trouble?" Stanley reached into his shirt pocket and removed the handkerchief to clean his glasses once again.

"He didn't show up for the first day of summer classes."

"Shouldn't you be talking with the chair of his department?"

"I did."

"And he told you to come see me?" The handkerchief faltered briefly before resuming its work.

"Nothing like that. He gave me access to Professor Rigby's files. Unofficial access, of course. The professor took daily notes and I noticed that he spent an inordinate amount of time here at the museum. I was hoping you might have noticed something."

"Noticed something?"

"Maybe any unusual behavior. Comments about his work. Relationship trouble. I don't have many leads at the moment."

"Then you have *some* leads?"

The urgency of the question surprised Toozie, and she said, "Not necessarily leads. More like speculations. We think he may have gone to Baja on a last-minute fishing trip. It's quite possible he broke down somewhere and is without means to communicate."

"He does like to fish," the curator agreed. He reset his glasses and carefully folded the handkerchief. He seemed to relax slightly as he placed it back into his pocket.

"Was he acting unusual in any way the last time he was here?" Toozie asked for the second time in as many minutes.

Stanley looked up from the desk as if coming out of deep thought. "Strange? No, I wouldn't say that. Maybe a bit preoccupied with work. But professors get that way before classes start up."

"When did you last see him?"

"Oh, it's been quite a while. A few weeks at least."

Toozie saw his eyes flit toward the window and then back again. She said, "The young woman out front, the receptionist, said Mr. Rigby was here just the other day. The sign-in log shows he checked out an old Jesuit trunk."

"I'm not surprised. Digby's always digging around in the undocumented artifacts room. He's an expert in the Jesuit missions of Baja California."

"Digby?"

"Duncan Rigby. But he goes by Digby." Stanley stood. "Well, if you don't have any more questions, Ms. McGill, I'd like to get back to work."

"I'm curious…" Toozie said. "That rather large book to the left of the cookbooks." She pointed at the shelves behind him.

Stanley turned and Toozie reached down and adhered a tiny listening device to the underside of her chair.

The curator turned back around. "*Jesuit Missions in Baja California*," he said. "A classic in the genre."

"It's just that you said you specialized in coins and metals. Were the Jesuits known for such things?"

Stanley gave a tight shrug. "Some metallurgy. Placer mines mostly. A few *hornitos* have been found around some of the missions."

"*Hornitos?*"

"Little furnaces. Adobe kilns used to smelt ore."

"I see."

"I've been stuck here for a long time, Ms. McGill. Mexico's just down the way. Such proximity to the border all these years has piqued my interest in many things Baja-related."

"When in Rome," Toozie said earnestly and stood from her chair. "Thank you for your time."

Stanley walked her to the door. He held it open, and she turned and handed him a business card. "If you think of anything that might help our search for Duncan…Digby, please call me, day or night."

Stanley glanced down at the card. "Of course," he said without looking up. "Of course."

CHAPTER TWENTY-FIVE

Punta Baja, Baja California Sur

An hour after dropping the twins at the dock, Molly anchored the schooner near Punta Baja's abandoned fish camp. Digby readied the dinghy and by late afternoon the two were working their way up the dirt path toward the cave.

Molly slowed. "You managed to get a trunk filled with gold and silver all the way up here?"

"We ferried it in tackle boxes. Took a couple dozen trips with Jack helping. His brother was in no shape to do much. Then we hauled up the trunk with what was left inside."

She scanned the hillside. "It'll be dark soon. You're not worried about the raccoon returning to its cave?"

"I don't think he's coming back anytime soon. Not with the smell of humans and gunpowder in there."

They walked in silence with Digby in front and Molly following a few body lengths behind. As they approached the cave entrance Digby slowed.

"What is it?" Molly asked.

"Something's wrong." He knelt and surveyed the ground. "These gouges are fresh. They weren't here earlier." He glanced around. "But they disappear almost as quickly as they start."

Molly inspected the marks in the dirt. "Like something heavy was dragged out to here."

"Shit."

She eyed him doubtfully.

"Someone tried to drag the trunk from the cave. They must have emptied it and then carried it off."

"I had a feeling your tale was too good to be true."

Digby hurried inside the cave, and emerged seconds later with a single pearl-encrusted rosary. He caught up with her and said, "Whoever it was must have been in a hell of a hurry to drop this and not notice."

Molly's eyes widened. "You must have been watched," she said, caressing the old pearls.

"By who?"

"Someone on a boat with binoculars, maybe."

"There wasn't a boat anywhere. I was looking. Hoping someone would pull into the bay so I could get away from my idiot kidnappers. But the horizon was empty until you showed up." Digby punched the air angrily.

She turned the palm-size cross over and ran her fingers along the rough edges. "It's heavier than I expected. Is it just silver?"

Digby chewed thoughtfully on his mustache. "The process was less refined back then. Silver and gold were contaminated with other alloys even after the smelting process. Nothing like the sterling silver most people are used to today."

Molly handed back the rosary. "If it wasn't a boat, then whoever took the treasure must have been here when you and the twins arrived."

"The fish camp is deserted."

"Not to mention that this is one of the least attractive bays in this stretch of Baja. No sand beach, no decent road in, nothing. The odds that someone drove in here during the last few hours and happened upon that cave filled with treasure are all but impossible."

Digby gave a dejected nod.

"Which is good news."

"It is?"

"It means whoever it was must live around here. And that gives us a chance of finding him."

"The only people who live around here are the *pangeros* who come and go with the fishing season. Like I said, they abandoned camp weeks ago."

"I'd bet my boat someone lives up in these hills. Baja is a magnet for pioneers and loners. Expatriates running from the law, locals running from the law, the law running from the law. Not to mention your run-of-the-mill misanthropes, recluses, and weirdos. Hell, I wouldn't be surprised if there's more than one cave dweller hiding in this mountain range. This stretch of coastline's perfect for wanderers and vagabonds."

Digby pocketed the rosary. "I hope you're right." He looked up at the sky, and tugged at the sides of his mustache. "Sun's about to drop behind the mountain. Too late to search for our hermit."

"There's an extra berth on board. It's a bit cramped in the fantail but you're welcome to it."

"My truck's still down there. I can sleep in the cab and start the search in the morning."

Molly reached back and tightened her braid. "I wouldn't have offered if I didn't want the company. Besides, two lowlifes already tracked you down the peninsula, kidnapped you, and stole your treasure. They had to be working for someone. Someone who might still show up. You're safer on the boat."

"Hanging around me seems to be dangerous. You'll be safer alone."

"Then we'll sail her farther offshore for the night." She paused and then said, "I was raised around more danger than most people see in a lifetime. My parents were gypsies. Pacifists who wanted to save the world. We sailed to every port in crisis as I was growing up. And I'm not talking about friendly banana republics. I'm talking places you're told never to go. Places like Angola, Liberia, Burma, Colombia, South Africa. Even China. Do you know what it takes to be a nonviolent activist in those places? My parents were fearless. They followed Gandhi's teachings. They believed that the wisdom of nonviolence lies in every heart—even the hearts of the most atrocious despots."

"You said 'were.' Are they—?"

"Disappeared," Molly said, finishing his sentence. "In Brazil two years ago, while fighting for landless peasants. I was away at college. Studying human rights at the University of Peace in Costa Rica. I took a leave of absence and went looking for them. But I didn't find them. The peasants said they were killed. I didn't believe it at first. But after a year I had to get on with my life. Their sailboat was still docked in Campeche, so I set off to plan the rest of my life. That was almost a year ago."

"I'm sorry," Digby said.

"If they did die, they lived the life they wanted. And I know they died doing something important. So this treasure hunt we're about to go on? It, too, is important. To you and to the world. It might be dangerous, but it doesn't scare me."

"I wish I could say the same."

"*Juntos*," she said, and held out her hand.

Digby took it. "A team, then."

"A team," she agreed, and led him down the path to the waiting dinghy.

CHAPTER TWENTY-SIX

Baja California Sur

Fish retraced his route from Ronald Stump's mega-yacht beyond the sailboats moored in La Paz Bay and was soon airborne, flying low between the island of Espíritu Santo and the road to the salt pans of San Evaristo. In the distance the island of San José loomed against a topaz sky. A light headwind teased the sea below, and Fish could see a mother whale shark and her pup rolling in a school of krill.

He placed a John Prine CD into its slot beneath the dashboard and perfected a slow circle above the whale sharks. He slid open the Plexiglas window and waited as the afternoon sun angled behind him. The sea below seemed to crystallize in the light, and he dropped in low and aimed a camera out the window. As he clicked a series of photographs, John Prine and Bonnie Raitt sang a duet about an angel from Montgomery.

Fish beamed as he banked back on course, and for the next two hours connected the island dots of Santa Cruz, Monserrat, Carmen, and eventually San Marcos and the humpbacked dome of Isla Tortuga. A small pod of killer whales slowed him just outside Bahía Concepcíon, and twice he veered inland to inspect abandoned fish camps with their cactus-ribbed drying racks and tar-paper shacks. Mostly, though, the flight was filled with vistas of sparkling blue water marred by the occasional sportfisher or the gust of an afternoon breeze.

By five o'clock he was over the famous port town of Santa Rosalia, established in 1884 by a French copper-mining company.

Its architecture was the most unique in all of Baja, with clapboard houses and a metal church designed by Gustave Eiffel. Fish had visited Santa Rosalia many times, mostly for the French bakery, which offered the best *pan dulce* on the peninsula.

Fish felt a twinge of hunger and angled toward the marina, tempted to land and load up on the famous bread, when the sun dropped below the peak of the Tres Virgenes. Lengthening shadows would only hinder his search for the missing archaeologist, so he banked back on course and was soon following the main dirt road into the mountain range. No vehicles traversed the rugged passage and there were no signs of a disabled truck or stranded archaeologist anywhere. There were no wandering cattle, no vultures, nothing but tumbleweeds and rocks and the occasional withering cactus.

As Fish climbed, he marveled at the beauty of the obsidian hillsides. The wide swaths of lava coursing downward split off and spread like the spanned wings of a giant raven. Elephant trees stippled the rugged landscape, interspersed among the low-lying brittle bush and creosote. He spotted some of Baja's few remaining ironwood trees tucked into the broken, dried magma, safe from the axes of local artisans who would gladly carve the branches into sailfish and sea turtles and arcing dolphins.

The old road coursed the mountain and then dropped down toward a rugged arroyo and into a remote, boulder-strewn bay. Through the plane's windshield, he could see the darkening Sea of Cortez. He grabbed a pair of binoculars, and as he descended, he spotted a restored schooner sailing off in the distance. It was tacking in the late afternoon breeze, and Fish could see its expansive teakwood deck and prominent maidenhead.

As he neared the craft, he saw that the carved bowsprit was made of solid dark wood, formed into a perfect replica of the Greek goddess Medusa. Only instead of a visage of villainy, she portrayed uncanny joy. An almost mischievous light to her wooden eyes. He could just make out the female sailor as she turned the boat, allowing him to catch the name painted at the stern: *Taliswoman*. He made a mental note to look her up should he ever need a shipwright to restore a future purchase. Maybe moor an old classic in the shallows in front of Cantina del Cielo. Add a little pirate romance to the view from the bar.

He was scanning the surrounding water and then the shoreline when his pulse quickened. Upside down in the surf was a pickup, its wheels washed clean by the crashing waves. A second pickup sat upright fifty yards above the shoreline, its hood stuck between a boulder and a mesquite whose spindly arms wrapped around an empty metal rack and an equally empty bed.

The brown sands of the surrounding arroyo glistened with the tributaries of an earlier rainstorm. Fish circled low and aimed his camera. The sun had long disappeared behind the mountains, but enough lambent light remained to focus on the Arizona license plate.

He circled again, this time searching for signs of the drivers or their passengers. All he saw were vestiges of an old fish camp, and a pair of caracaras resting atop two saguaro-like *cardónes*. Fish snapped a few photos, and then dialed Toozie's number from the plane's satellite telephone.

"McGill Detective Agency."

"Toozie, it's me. I think I found the truck. No sign of the archaeologist, but a pickup matching the description is stuck in an arroyo near Punta Baja. The skiff is missing, but there's a rack that might have held one. And Arizona plates."

"Punta Baja?"

"A stretch of rocky beach at the coastal foot of the Tres Virgenes. I'm looking at an arroyo with a seasonal fish camp."

"Did you get the license number on the truck?"

Fish lifted the camera from his lap and scrolled through the photos. He zoomed in on the license plate. "Ready?"

He read the number to Toozie.

"Bingo. Was it abandoned?"

"I think so," Fish said. "But there's a wrinkle."

"Okay."

"A second pickup had washed down the arroyo and flipped in the surf."

There was a pause.

"I didn't see any bodies, though. Which doesn't mean our client's not lodged inside the swamped truck."

"Or the twins who followed him to Baja."

"Kidnappers?"

"Looks that way."

"Somebody knew he'd find the treasure?"

Toozie took a deep breath and explained, "I met with the museum curator here in Tucson a few hours ago. A man named Stanley Cohen. He was trying hard not to be nervous. Too hard. I planted a listening device before I left."

"You bugged the office?"

"And heard him make a phone call minutes after I left. He was scared. He called a man in Long Beach, California. I ran the man's name."

"Let me guess. Another treasure hunter."

"An art thief. Priors for stolen Aztec and Mayan collectibles. Before that it was rare coins. He did a stint at Lompoc, just north of Santa Barbara. Apparently, he's working as a security guard at the Museum of Latin American Art. Under a fake identity, of course."

"I thought you said the archaeologist was followed from *Tucson*."

"Originally, yes. The curator had him followed by a couple of deadbeats named Zack and Jack. From what I could gather from the call, they were supposed to steal the treasure from Digby, leave him out in the desert, and then bring the treasure back to Stanley, who was planning to announce the find to the world. I imagine he's been watching Digby for a long time, in case the archaeologist found something. Anyway, Stanley was livid about losing touch with the twins. Said they should have never double-crossed him."

"And now this art thief is heading my way?"

"Not exactly."

"The curator?"

She laughed. "He's not the type. A man named Slim."

"Slim?"

"The brother of our art thief. And an expert in finding missing people."

"A bounty hunter."

"That's my guess."

Fish rubbed his eyes and let his hand drop to the tip of his goatee. "So this Digby is either dead or wandering around the mountains somewhere. Meanwhile, our twins may or may not be alive based on the state of the trucks. The treasure could be anywhere, and now we've got a professional heading down to clean up the mess."

"A bounty hunter with dollar signs in his eyes."

"Right."

"Which is why he'll be armed and extremely dangerous."

"When do you think he crossed the border?"

"Maybe yesterday."

Fish exhaled. "I'm headed back to Mag Bay now. I'll recruit a friend and grab some heavy artillery and head back here first thing in the morning. If the archaeologist is alive, we'll find him."

"I've booked a flight to Long Beach tonight. I plan to drop by the Museum of Latin American Art in the morning. Start some dialogue with this art thief. Mention my sudden interest in the Jesuit Treasure. Stir up the hornets. Then I'll catch the afternoon flight to Loreto. Rent a car and head to Punta Baja."

"It might be better if you stayed north of the border. At least until we clear out this Slim character."

"I'm no desert rose, Francis. My client's in serious trouble. Men with guns are part of the game."

"Which is why Skegs and I will be back at first light. We'll snoop around. See where the tracks lead. Skegs is a local. He knows people. Old-timers. Cops. He'll spread the word about Slim the bounty hunter. In the meantime, maybe you can dig up more information about him. If he's checking in with his brother in Long Beach, you might be able to get a location on him. I'd sure like to know how close he is."

"Call me if you find anything."

"Like a few million in gold and silver washed down that arroyo?"

"In that case, I want photos."

Fish laughed, his green eyes flashing. "I'm glad you're coming down."

There was a pause, and Toozie said, "I sent your cell phone some photos. A couple of recent head shots of Digby." There was a longer pause. "In case he's unable to identify himself."

"We'll find him, Toozie."

"That's not what I'm afraid of."

"I'll be careful."

"Will you?"

"The greedy make mistakes. I've got more money than I'll ever need. And I don't believe in celestial good fortune. Or bad. I couldn't care less about this treasure, and that gives me a hell of an advantage over the bad guys."

"I hope you're right."

"I've also got an incentive they don't."

"What's that?"

"You."

CHAPTER TWENTY-SEVEN

Santa Rosalia, Baja California Sur

Slim Dixon awoke from his nap after feasting on lobster burritos at Mama Espinoza's Restaurant, and then drove the six hours to Guerrero Negro, where he ate a midnight dinner of huevos rancheros at the tourist-friendly Malarrimo Restaurant. After that he filled up his truck at the all-night Pemex station down the street, where fluent Spanish and an extra hundred pesos confirmed the recent visit of a trio of Americans, one driving alone in a tan F-150 with an aluminum skiff on the rack, the other two—twin brothers—following closely behind in an old Toyota.

Three hours later, Slim swung into San Ignacio and stopped briefly at one of Baja's most famous missions, hoping for a public restroom. Finding the arched doorway locked, he tucked into a shadow beside a stone wall and relieved himself.

On his way back to the Cadillac, he shined a pocket flashlight over the elaborate three-story facade and noticed the four friars carved from stone. All four were depicted on pedestals and inset into the towering wall. One, however, stood out above all the rest. It wasn't just that the statue hovered above the lower friars, or that it stood closest to the steeple, with its ancient bronze bell colored green with patina. What made this particular priest stand out was what he was missing. Whether the bust had purposely been desecrated or whether Mother Nature had guillotined it, Slim didn't know. But to Slim, the image of a headless priest on the wall of such a holy site was more than illustrative. It was a prophecy. He couldn't help but think that the Jesuit had been beheaded for his participation in the theft of the treasure from the king of Spain. A powerful sign for a man of Slim's profession.

The hit man clicked off the light. Slim returned to his convertible with a sudden acuteness to his senses. He leapt over the closed car door and bounced onto the front seat.

At three in the morning, San Ignacio was empty as a graveyard. He clasped his hands behind his head and stared up at the night sky, hardly noticing the sea of stars. He could feel the excitement burrowing up from his loins. A pleasant churning in his gut.

He'd felt it lingering since crossing into the southern state of Baja a few hours earlier, and he knew it would only strengthen in intensity now that he'd seen his vision. Now that he was near the famed missions whose lore had attracted treasure hunters for centuries. Treasure hunters like the archaeologist and the fools who tracked him. Slim knew he would find them soon. Knew they were close. His visions never failed him. "Hallelujah," he heard himself utter.

He started the engine and drove around the *zócalo*, the headlights from the Cadillac casting odd shadows across the mature laurel trees. A homeless man slept on a bench curled beneath a colorful Mexican blanket, his filthy bare feet exposed. Slim wondered if a bullet to the head might be a blessing for the man. The thought intrigued him, and he reached for the gun, slowing the Cadillac, when he noticed the police car parked across the street. Its interior light was dark and it seemed unoccupied, but Slim knew it was another sign.

Keep moving.

He set down the gun and rounded the *zócalo*. He headed back to the highway driving fast, adrenaline pushing him to the edge of recklessness. An hour later, the sky began to lighten. In the distance, the Sea of Cortez appeared like a specter in the approaching dawn. Slim descended the steep grade toward Santa Rosalia as if brakes were meant for mortals, slowing only once to take in the view of the sea. He wondered if the archaeologist had been tempted to veer toward the coast for a swim. After hours of traversing endless desert and unforgiving asphalt, Slim was tempted to do the same. Pause in the warm sea and purify his journey. But the voice whispered in his ear:

Keep moving.

He checked the pistol for the umpteenth time, tucked it into his waistband, and pulled off the highway at the Pemex just outside of town.

"*Hola compadre*," he said to the gas station attendant as he parked beside a green gas pump. "*Lleno por favor.*"

The attendant nodded.

Slim reached into his wallet and pulled out a hundred-peso note. "I was wondering," he continued in Spanish, "if you could help me find some friends. They left a few days ahead of me. One guy's driving a truck with an aluminum skiff on top. The other two are following him in an old Toyota pickup. Twin brothers driving."

The attendant took the bill and shook his head. "Haven't seen them, amigo."

Slim tilted back his cowboy hat. "First guy has a shark tooth tattooed down his arm. Big one. Medium-build with a blond mustache."

The attendant shook his head again.

"The other two are stocky. Identical twins with greasy hair, T-shirts, baseball caps. One guy spitting tobacco juice all the time."

"Nope."

The two men stared at each other until Slim wondered why the attendant hadn't started filling the car with gas.

"You sure you haven't seen them."

"I'm sure, señor."

A vein in Slim's temple twitched. He reached into his wallet and removed a second hundred-peso note.

The man smiled. He reached out and took the money. "But I know someone who has seen them. Yesterday afternoon. An American couple came into the harbor on a sailboat. The man had a big shark tooth tattooed down his arm. He and the girl dropped two gringos at the dock. Twins. Both were injured. The tattooed man gave the dockmaster twenty bucks for a taxi to take them to the hospital. Then he boarded the sailboat and left with the redhead."

"That's a lot of information."

"It's not every day a guy with no ears gets dropped off at the dock."

"No ears?"

The attendant shrugged.

"And the brother?" Slim asked sardonically. "He have any ears?"

"Sí. But only one eye. *El Chupacabra...*" His voice trailed off as if mention of the mythical monster might bring a similar fate.

Slim narrowed his gaze. "Do you take me for a fool?"

"No señor. It is true. The dockmaster's my brother. He drove them to the hospital himself."

"What hospital?"

The attendant pointed. "Two stoplights. Turn right. It's up the hill. Near the top." He started to unscrew the Cadillac's gas cap.

Slim turned toward the car.

"Forget the gas," Slim said and slammed the car into gear and sped from the gas station toward town.

CHAPTER TWENTY-EIGHT

Cabo San Lucas, Baja California Sur

At four in the morning, Barbie passed through the French doors of the mega-yacht's salon like an albino thrust into sunlight. She wore a baggy, colorless, one-piece jumpsuit, black Doc Martens, and a pair of lambskin gloves. Her head was cloaked in a white turban. As extra precautions, she'd added wraparound sunglasses and a satin shawl wet with antibacterial spray that encircled her nose and mouth. A smokeless cigarette with an elongated plastic filter extended from a hole in the shawl.

"The maid disinfected the entire room less than thirty minutes ago," Stump assured her through an intercom. His image appeared on a wall-size flat-screen television.

"A small gesture, considering the risks," Barbie muttered through the wraps of satin.

"I won't waste more of your time than I must," Stump continued. "My sources tell me you've made a substantial offer for the Jesuit Treasure. I'm prepared to pay you a million in cash to become uninterested. In the satchel on the table." He pointed a finger and Barbie followed it from the screen to a glass coffee table across the room. "The satchel has also been washed and disinfected. The cash, I'm afraid, has not, but you'll have to trust me on the amount. Have your people count it later."

Barbie puffed at her plastic cigarette, removed it with a gloved hand, and said, "The million is a nice gesture, Ronald. But we both know the treasure holds far more worth than mere currency."

"Yes, but my offer comes risk-free."

"Are you a superstitious man?"

Stump considered the question and said, "My beliefs are irrelevant. You went to the trouble of coming here. Why?"

Barbie released a sparrow's laugh and glanced around the room. "A fine collection of rare art. Your dealer must be exquisitely positioned."

"None better."

"Flattery will get you nowhere."

Stump said nothing.

Barbie continued, "It appears that Harvey Dixon is playing the field. He called Charlie Diamond, another of my customers, and offered him the treasure for twenty million."

"Mr. Diamond is an amateur."

"That he is. But his money is as green as ours."

Barbie carefully rethreaded the plastic cigarette filter through the opening in the shawl and made a sucking sound. "Will you be coming to the club tonight?" she asked, her voice taking on its familiar lilt. "Las Margaritas is dancing. Unless she has a better offer, of course."

"Two million and you walk away," Stump said impatiently. "The second million deposited directly into your Caribbean account the minute I have the treasure on board. The million in the satchel you may take with you tonight. As another gesture of my good faith."

Barbie stepped lightly to the table and lifted the satchel with a gloved hand. "A most generous offer," she said and turned back toward the French doors. She paused and lowered the satchel to the carpet. "All this excitement and I almost forgot. Charlie Diamond is being blackmailed."

"Blackmailed?"

"I have little birds everywhere, Ronald. You of all people should know that." She puffed dramatically on the filter. "Two of them hit the jackpot yesterday. A routine art theft I arranged seems to have uncovered a dirty little secret kept by Charles. He's desperate now. It might be wise to remember that the foolhardy are prone to delusion. Charles, I expect, shall overplay his hand."

Barbie tilted her head toward the ceiling and blew invisible smoke rings into the air. "The cursed crown, if it exists, is priceless. Charlie Diamond will never have it. Nor will you. The rest is, of course, negotiable."

Stump saw the shawl undulate around her chin, and he wondered if the woman was smiling or yawning. He was about to respond when she said, "I believe you have a bodyguard that used to wrestle on TV."

Stump waited.

"He came into the club earlier this evening. Curious about an expatriate living in Magdalena Bay. I loaned him a Range Rover. I hope you don't mind. Seems Mr. Hissken was intent on revisiting a certain discussion he had with the man aboard this very yacht."

Stump's face reddened. "Meddling in Mr. Diamond's affairs is one thing, Barbie, but do not interfere with mine."

Barbie waved a glove through the air. "Interfere? I only want to help rid you of your little distractions."

"Rid me?"

"An untraceable gun in the glove compartment of the Range Rover, for starts. In case our man required more than a bowie knife to make his impression." She sucked at the cigarette.

"Goddamn you," Stump growled. "Don't pretend like you're doing me any favors. Snake is no longer in my employ. What he does with that gun is *your* problem."

Barbie's left hand plucked the electronic cigarette from the opening in the shawl. "When your bodyguard returns, you may desire him to have a visit with Mr. Diamond. Reinforce my suggestion that Charles's need for the treasure is misplaced. Refocus his attention on his billboards. Unless he has an extra hundred million lying around, that is."

Stump stared savagely from the television screen.

"A pleasure doing business," Barbie said, and exited the yacht like a chimera in the night.

CHAPTER TWENTY-NINE

Magdalena Bay, Baja California Sur

Atticus Fish awoke before dawn at his sand dune island hideaway in preparation for his flight back across the peninsula to Punta Baja, where he planned to splash down and spend the day searching the hillsides for the missing archaeologist. He'd called Skegs the night before and arranged to meet the mescal salesman at Cantina del Cielo for a quick breakfast and a promise to buy an extra case of booze and all the phony ironwood carvings the man could make. Skegs may have been Fish's best friend, but friends had bills to pay.

After a thirty-minute swim off the bay side of the island followed by his daily routine of push-ups and sit-ups, Fish spent the next half hour filling the tanks of his seaplane's biodiesel engines with converted fish oil, purchased weekly from the nearby cannery. He spread fresh hay for Mephistopheles, and fed the two Labrador retrievers, Sting and Ray. Then he hurried into his four-story driftwood home for a jug of water and homemade fish jerky. Flight snacks.

The driftwood house was built in the shape of an octagon and was nestled into a canyon of sand between the Pacific Ocean and one of the many Magdalena back bays. Made from planking salvaged from an old shipwreck and locally fired adobe bricks, the residence was a marvel of engineering. The octagonal shape held back the continuously shifting sands, and was anchored by an eighty-foot redwood tree barged down from Malarrimo and sunk twenty feet deep. Attached to the tree were rough-hewn beams extending outward to each of the eight walls in a wagon-wheel pattern.

The bottom floor was driftwood set in a herringbone pattern and packed with beach sand. A spiral iron staircase coiled up the tree, allowing access to eight rope bridges leading to eight separate rooms. Above the rooms was a turret-style balcony that overlooked both the Pacific and the back bay. And above that a wide balcony with a tightly woven *palapa* held off the intense winter winds.

The outer walls of the home were decorated with dozens of salvaged nautical windows green with patina. Glass fishing floats the size of party balloons hung from old fishing nets draped like shutters bracketing each round window. A rope-ladder walkway led from the top porch down a football field of sloping sand to the shores of the Pacific Ocean. On the bay side, a clamshell path meandered through the dunes toward the placid inner waters, where it branched off to an airplane-size garage with a camouflage awning.

Fish loaded the water and jerky into a backpack, and took the clamshell path through the sand dunes to the garage, set low to the rising sand. The structure had been paneled in cactus ribs and then drenched in tack and blanketed in sand. The roofline of the hangar was malleable tin fashioned into rolling peaks and valleys to mimic the surrounding terrain. The tin had also been coated with tack and sprinkled with sand. The effect was a near perfect mirage, especially when viewed by curious boaters cruising the inner bay or the occasional shell seeker wandering the inner beach. A necessary precaution for a man of Fish's background.

Inside the garage were ATVs in various states of repair, a pair of four-stroke personal watercraft, a super panga, enough dive gear to outfit a platoon of Navy SEALs, spearguns, Hawaiian slings, an array of fishing and hunting knives, miscellaneous rods and reels, surfboards, and two kayaks fitted with trolling gear. But Fish wasn't there for beach toys this morning. He'd come for the small arsenal of firearms. Weaponry hidden beneath a trapdoor that in turn was hidden beneath a pair of off-road vehicles.

Fish rolled the ATVs toward the corner of the room, freed the trapdoor, and stepped down into a small basement. Shadowy light filtered down onto racked rifles and pistols lining one of the wood-paneled walls. Opposite the firearms were machetes, a few swords, and a large collection of skinning knives. The third wall displayed an eclectic array of blowguns, a scythe, and a handful of martial arts stars. But it was the fourth wall that Fish focused on. A framed Baja map the size of a refrigerator was affixed to it. Fish ran his fingers along the edge of the map and felt the three dials countersunk into the frame. He turned each dial by memory, spread his arms wide from top to bottom, and pressed down the two steel pegs. He heard the click of the steel frame unlatching, and watched it slowly swing open.

Fish stepped into the vault and waited for the motion detector to light his surroundings. The smell of the past engulfed him as he moved quickly toward ten columns of shrink-wrapped hundred-dollar bills rising nearly seven feet high. Each column contained a hundred stacks, and each stack was worth ten thousand dollars. Ten million total. A small fraction of his net worth hidden around the world. Tucked beneath the sands of Isla Santo Domingo. Petty cash for an expatriate in hiding. Emergency funds for the ex-attorney. Insurance against the verisimilitudes of fanatics who wanted him dead.

Ransom for an archaeologist he'd never met.

He stuffed a million into a knapsack and backed from the vault. He swung the heavy door back into place and spun the dials until the pegs latched. Then he lifted two pistols from the wall and climbed from the basement. He reset the trapdoor, the oil-soaked carpet, and the ATVs, and ten minutes later was lifting off from the slick waters of the bay. He soared over the snake's nest of mangroves and turned toward the port town of San Carlos, fifteen minutes away.

On the horizon he could just make out sailboats listing with the outgoing tide, their hulls shiny and white against the turquoise bay. With binoculars he saw the outline of the chili-green Cantina del Cielo, where Skegs would be waiting with two plates of huevos rancheros and a steaming mug of fresh-brewed coffee. Probably sharing a side of home fries with the hungover iguanas, Pancho and Lefty. Ignoring the squawks of Chuy, the scarlet macaw, high in the rafters of the open-air bar.

Fish set the binoculars on the copilot seat and wondered if Toozie would enjoy scratching the head of a drunken iguana. He was smiling at the thought when he noticed a plume of dust rising from the dirt road leading to the fish camp across the bay from his home. A Range Rover was speeding north toward the shoreline of beached pangas, a dozen or so canoelike boats fitted with outboards capable of crossing the narrow back bay within minutes. Fish raised the binoculars from the passenger seat and felt his jaw tighten.

Snake Hissken.

The knife-loving Jesus freak had one hand on the steering wheel. The other hung from the driver-side window, its bicep adorned with a snake coiling down to a familiar pair of bloody fangs.

CHAPTER THIRTY

Santa Rosalia, Baja California Sur

Slim parked the convertible Cadillac in the hospital patient lot and entered the emergency wing of the hospital. It was just past dawn, and the nurse rotation was still a few hours away. The overnight crew was finalizing paperwork, checking drip bags, and brewing fresh coffee to stay awake. Slim strolled to the check-in counter.

"Good morning," he said with a deep southern drawl meant to charm the middle-aged nurse.

She eyed him warily until he slipped into fluent Spanish explaining how he'd driven all the way from Arizona upon hearing that his younger twin brothers had been injured in a bizarre double attack. Something about missing eyes and ears. How their mother back in Dallas was worried sick. Then he passed her three hundred pesos and a million-dollar smile. Minutes later he was strolling down the hall toward the recovery wing of the hospital. Room 101.

Two beds, two brothers.

Zack and Jack.

The Santa Rosalia hospital was unusually state-of-the-art for Baja California, especially considering the town's lack of tourism. The floors gleamed with fresh wax, and the walls were freshly painted and hung with colorful ocean murals. Something Slim might have expected in the tourist towns of Cabo San Lucas or La Paz, but not in a town littered with the rusting relics of its mining heritage.

But Santa Rosalia had always been a Baja anomaly. From its classic French bakeries to its European-style architecture and imported, hand-stamped tin church, the city always managed to attract just enough tourists to survive. The recent completion of a new marina, with its inviting ferry dock and clean restaurants, was attracting more and more mainlanders. Foreigners redis-covering the offshore islands of Tortuga and San Marcos, where anglers and divers enjoyed a plethora of year-round yellowtail and lobster along with the summertime bonus of dorado and sailfish.

Which accounted for the new Pemex just outside of town. And the modernized hospital with the portable MED machine Slim saw resting on a four-wheeled cart beneath a painting of a Sea of Cortez sunset. A state-of-the-art manual external defibril-lator, resembling an old IBM desktop computer. Twenty pounds of electronic heart starter, like those found in hospitals across America. A swift thousand volts of electricity to restart the ticker. Or better yet, to stimulate the memory of taciturn hostages. Slim yanked the defibrillator from the cart and entered room 101.

The man lying on the far bed was snoring softly, his head shaved and his ears covered in bundles of gauze. White surgical tape held the oversize earmuffs in place, crisscrossing his hair-less pate. A plastic tube ran from his arm to a clear bag that hung from a rack beside the bed. A thin sheet covered the snoring man's legs.

The near bed held an equally peculiar sight. A man laying awake with one eye covered in a patch held in place by tape run-ning from beneath his chin to the crown of his head and back again. The one-eyed man was shirtless and wore a pair of salt-stained blue jeans. The man's working eye blinked wide with con-fusion and fright.

Slim unclipped the two defibrillator paddles from the MED. He raised one to the brim of his cowboy hat and tipped it back with a brief nod. He dropped his hand and switched on the con-trol dial of the battery pack. A high-pitched whine filled the room.

One-eye sat up quickly.

Slim placed a finger across his lips.

"Who the hell are *you*?" the man demanded.

Slim took a lunging step and said, "One more word and you'll beg your maker to hold your tongue."

One-eye grabbed a pillow and bear-hugged it. "Sorry."

Slim scowled. He leaned forward, touched the paddles to the dimwit's bare feet, and pressed the hand trigger. The paddles buzzed with a jolt of electricity.

One-eye's legs stiffened like a pennant in the wind. His back arched and his mouth opened, but no sound emerged. Then his eye closed and he slumped sideways and passed out.

When Jack came to, he was lying across the backseat of a moving convertible, the morning sun warm on the leather interior.

In the front seat was his brother Zack, perched upright, one of the defibrillator paddles affixed to his carotid artery by a strip of silver duct tape. The other paddle was in the hand of the driver in the cowboy hat, a hand draped across Zack's shoulders. The cowboy drummed the paddle across the back of Zack's neck in rhythm with a Tom Petty song blaring from the Cadillac's sound system.

Jack sat up and blinked his one eye at the driver, who was watching him in the rearview mirror.

You don't have to live like a refugee…

Slim turned down the music. "One wrong move," he said, "and your brother gets a thousand volts to the brain stem. You think he's stupid now, just try something heroic."

"Who *are* you?"

"You already asked me that."

"What the hell do you want?"

"Directions."

"Directions where?"

"To the archaeologist and my treasure."

CHAPTER THIRTY-ONE

Magdalena Bay, Baja California Sur

Fish dropped the binoculars to his lap and grabbed his cell phone from the console beside the pilot seat.

"Skegs, I—" he started to say when his friend cut him off.

"For an ex-boxer, ex-American, ex-fisherman, ex-everything, you sure know how to hire a cook, man. These huevos rancheros are supremo!"

"Glad you—"

"Dude," he continued through a mouthful of food. "You should bottle this recipe. Call it *Huevos Fantasticos*. I'll sell it with my mescal. Down in Cabo and La Paz. It'll become Baja's cure to the hangover. Gringos are gonna love it, bro!"

"Skegs, I need you to go into my back office and get on the radio and call the guys at the fish camp. Tell them—"

"Whoa, slow down, Captain America. First off, I can hear the engines in the background, so I know you're on your way. Second off, did I mention these eggs? I just ordered a second plate. On the house, of course."

"You can have all the eggs you want. But right now I need your help. We have a sudden and very serious issue."

"Only issue I've got is an expanding stomach."

"There's a guy in a Range Rover speeding toward the fish camp. The same man I knocked unconscious yesterday on Stump's yacht in La Paz. He's dangerous."

"Man, why didn't you say something?"

"I've been trying."

"No, I mean earlier. You can't go around beating the bejesus out of people and not telling your wingman. That's when things like this happen."

"Things like what?"

"Miscommunication, man. I need to be in the loop so we don't spend all our time jawing about eggs and shit."

"I've been a bit preoccupied lately."

"Still trying to impress that PI?"

Fish ignored the question. "Listen, call the fish camp and tell whoever you get on the radio to agree to take the man with the snake tattoos and bowie knives to my island. But tell him to fake engine trouble halfway across. Kink the fuel line. Whatever."

"Snake tattoos and bowie knives?"

"I'll explain later. And while you're in the office I also need you to dig around in the closet where I store my fishing tackle."

"You mean that crappy, old, broken-down stuff?"

Fish started his descent toward the flat water in front of his bar. "Behind all that stuff is a blowgun. About three feet long. Made of animal bone. Tufts of fur are still attached. You can't miss it. I need it."

"*Chupacabra* fur?"

"I'm serious, Skegs."

"Heading back there now."

"There's also a small red fly box in the top drawer of my desk. Grab that, too. But don't open it."

"Why the hell not?"

"Because the darts inside are coated with puffer fish toxin."

"You're shitting me."

"Dead serious."

"You're planning on killing this guy?"

"He took a swipe at Mephistopheles with a hunting knife. I had the feeling I was next. After I decked him, Stump warned me that I'd pay for the privilege with my life. I prefer not to take any chances."

"Murder's a hell of a payback."

"The toxin won't kill him. Just incapacitate him."

"Incapacitate? You said the guy has bowie knives. It *better* incapacitate him."

"Complete paralysis."

Fish heard Skegs opening a door. "Somehow I'd feel better with gunpowder and guns. Where you hiding them?"

"Firearms and booze don't mix."

"You don't drink."

"It's not me I'm worried about."

Scuffling noises came across the line and Skegs said, "Jesus, you weren't kidding about the fur. You sure this thing'll work?"

"I'm sure. Grab the red fly box and hurry."

"Then what?"

"Then we fly back and save a *pangero* before Snake slits his throat."

CHAPTER THIRTY-TWO

Punta Baja, Baja California Sur

Molly and Digby woke at first light, and after a hurried cup of coffee sailed back to Punta Baja and anchored and were soon at the *mapache* cave to begin their search. Molly had changed into beige board shorts and a long-sleeve running shirt. She wore a shrimp-colored visor Velcroed beneath her salmon-colored ponytail, and a pair of KEEN hiking sandals.

Digby's pair of jeans had dried overnight, along with the T-shirt he'd worn since discovering the treasure days earlier. Both were stiff with salt from the capsized skiff. He'd lost his wide-brimmed hat during the storm, and now wore a Taku River Reds baseball cap he'd found in Molly's spare bedroom.

After a cursory search of the cave, they split up and took opposite sides of the hillside, searching for signs of the treasure thief. Molly had gone left and Digby right when he made a gruesome discovery. Zack's other ear had shriveled under the summer air, and the decomposition had been hastened by a swarm of desert ants. As Digby bent down to retrieve it, he heard Molly call out from the rocks above him.

"The ridge!"

Digby looked up to see her pointing high up the hillside. A flash of sunlight reflected twice and then disappeared. A few seconds later, the double glint of sunshine reappeared.

"I think he's using binoculars," Digby said after scrambling to the rocks beside Molly. "Or maybe it's some sort of a signal." He adjusted his baseball cap and stared out to sea. "Except I don't see anything but your sailboat out there."

"I think the signal was for us," Molly said. "He knows we're here."

"He could have a telescope. The boat could be way out there."

"Only one way to find out."

"But why would our thief want *our* attention?"

"I don't know. But he waited until I was looking up there to send the signal. Then he waited for you to look up before he sent it again."

"Maybe it's a trap."

"Maybe, but that doesn't jibe either. Why expose his hiding place? He's way the hell up there. We never would have found him."

Digby thought for another moment and then said, "Except he knows I'd come back for the treasure. He saw me hide it. Maybe he wants to lure us up there and kill us. Keep it all for himself."

"Stealing's one thing, but double murder…" She shook her head. "Lying in wait? That's cold-blooded killer stuff."

"He just hit the lottery. Money like that can make a person do all kinds of things you'd never expect. Add the fact that he lives out here in the rocks and he's probably crazy to start with."

Molly gave a thoughtful nod and then said, "I like our odds. If he had a gun he'd have fired it already. If it's a trap, it'll most likely be a rockslide. We'll approach him from the far sides. I'll work my way farther left. You go as far right as you can. If he's planning to start an avalanche, it'll pass between us."

"We could go for help."

"And risk losing your once-in-a-lifetime find forever." She shook her head. "Stay away from any low areas. Keep to the bigger boulders. Places you can duck behind. In case he has a short-range weapon."

"Short-range weapon? Jesus, I can't believe this is happening."

Molly regarded him for a moment.

"It just seems so impossible," he added.

A double flash of sunlight caught their attention.

"He wants us to hurry," Molly said. She removed her backpack and reached inside. She handed Digby a flare gun. "Insurance," she said, and reslung the backpack over her shoulders.

"What about you?" he asked.

"I'll be okay."

Digby gave her a doubtful glance.

But Molly didn't explain. Another flash of sunlight sent her flitting across the slag like a lynx.

CHAPTER THIRTY-THREE

Baja California Sur

Slim drove along Highway 1 to the dirt turnoff into the Tres Virgenes mountain range. He followed Jack's directions, and thirty minutes later pulled into the arroyo leading to Punta Baja and stopped. His arm was still draped across Zack's shoulders, his finger hovering over the trigger of the defibrillator paddle. Zack stared wide-eyed through the dusty Cadillac windshield.

"Why are you stopping?" Jack asked, his voice raised in alarm, his working eye blinking rapidly.

"Change of plans."

"But you don't know where we hid the treasure."

"You said it was a cave at the end of the arroyo. Can't be too hard to find."

"Please don't kill us."

"Nobody's getting killed."

He pulled the trigger and watched Zack's head snap back, his body jerking spastically across the wide leather seat of the Cadillac. Seconds later the earless twin slumped forward and crumpled to the floorboards.

"Jesus, fuck!" Jack hollered, leaning forward with fists clenched. "Why'd you do that?"

Slim dropped the paddle, and in one smooth motion, without turning his head, aimed the pistol at Jack's chest. "Honoring that brotherly love."

Jack blinked blankly, his fists still clenched.

"Think about it, Einstein. Twins do everything together, right? Just look at the two of you. Both bandaged up. Both attacked by wild creatures. I figured it'd be unfair to zap one of you and not the other."

"That's fucked up."

"Call it family justice."

"It's still fucked up."

Zack began to moan from the footwell.

Slim motioned with the gun. "Get out and open the passenger door and help your brother up off the floor."

Jack followed instructions and helped Zack up to the seat, the second paddle still taped to his carotid artery.

"Now climb in between us."

"Why?"

Slim tilted back his Stetson with the barrel of the pistol. "Normally I wouldn't care who sits next to me." He wagged the gun again. "These armor-piercing bullets will go through the two of you like wax. And the car door and anything else that gets in the way. But unlike your brother, you have ears. It's dusty and hot, and I don't feel much like shouting this morning."

Digby and Molly approached a towering boulder near a labyrinth of ancient lava. At the top of the rock sat a dark-skinned man, cross-legged, his eyes closed, a mane of silver hair cascading down his naked chest. He was compact, with a flat nose and a wide, deeply tanned face. He wore a pair of crudely stitched pants that looked animal in origin, of earthen colors perfectly melding with the surrounding terrain. A set of bare feet that resembled slabs of dried fish covered with calluses as ridged and black as the surrounding parched magma moved to a silent rhythm. The man seemed to be in a trance.

Digby stopped. "In his hand," he whispered.

Molly nodded.

The man opened his eyes, and in the morning sun, his pupils flashed like matching circles of blue quartz. He raised the silver crown glistening with black pearls.

"*Magnífico*," he said in soft-spoken Spanish. Then in English, "I knew the legend was true."

"You speak English?" Digby replied.

"Some have searched for a lifetime," the man continued. "But few believe anymore." He lowered the crown to his lap. "Not after the rich white man searching for *El Dorado del Dios* found only cave art..." His voice trailed off.

"Erle Stanley Gardner?" Digby asked in astonishment.

The Indian's face took on a sudden vitality, as though Digby's words sparked a long forgotten memory.

"You knew him?"

The old man nodded.

Molly stepped forward. "You used the silver crown to signal us. Why?"

The Indian revealed a beautiful smile, his turquoise eyes drifting to Molly as he spoke. "This man was held hostage by two matching brothers with bad intentions. When he had the chance to escape, he took the captors with him. They were injured. Badly. He could have left them here to die. Instead, he abandoned the most famous treasure in all of Mexico." He turned to Digby. "My name is Pancho, and it is with great pleasure that we meet."

"I'm Digby, and this is my friend, Molly."

"*Mucho gusto.*"

"*Igualmente*," Molly replied. "But why did you signal us? You have the treasure. You could have kept it forever."

Before Digby could speak, Pancho said, "It is covered with the blood of my ancestors. Simple people who worshiped no idols. Foreign priests forced a strange religion on them with great violence. They knew nothing of Christ or his crown of thorns. But they gave the priests what they wanted…wealth. But this wealth does not belong to me. It does not belong to you. This crown has cursed the treasure for centuries." His eyes flitted toward the arroyo. "Those two men who held you hostage. The man who lost an eye? The other his ears? They were cursed, just like the Jesuits and those who came after. It is time the curse is broken." He raised the crown above his head and prepared to smash it upon the rocks.

"No!" Digby shouted.

Pancho stopped.

"Please. I am an archaeologist. The crown belongs to Mexico. Cursed or not, it should be preserved."

Molly watched in astonishment as the old man tossed the crown to Digby. "*Que le vaya bien*," he said and stood. "Someone is coming."

Digby caught the crown, spun on his feet, and followed Pancho's eyes toward the arroyo.

"Who?" Molly asked.

Digby stiffened.

Pancho motioned back up into the canyon. "In a moment you will see the dust. Then you must follow me."

"You left the rosary in the cave," Molly stated. "For us to find."

Pancho nodded.

Molly frowned. "But—"

"I knew he would return for the treasure. Mr. Digby needed to know it was taken by a caretaker, not some two-bit bandito. If not, he would have spent his life regretting kindness he offered to two men who would have killed him under different circumstances."

Molly was waiting for Digby to say something when the hermit pointed over their heads. "There," he said.

The two Americans turned and saw the cloud of dust rising near the far end of the arroyo.

"They may be tourists," Pancho said matter-of-factly, "or they may be looking for what you left behind."

"How often do you see tourists?" Digby asked.

"Never."

Digby pulled off his cap and took a long breath. He turned to Molly. "We need to go."

"There is a secret way," Pancho said. "A lava tube that emerges into the sea maybe a hundred meters north of the *mapache* cave. The climb down is dangerous, but I secured a rope for you. Trust it or you will get lost. When you emerge, swim to your boat. The sun is still rising so you can hide in the glare. But you must hurry before they see you."

Digby and Molly followed Pancho as he dropped from the boulder and into the maze of lava tubes.

"What about you?" Molly asked Pancho. "If they're after the treasure, they will search until they find it."

Pancho smiled widely. "But they will find the *mapache* cave empty. The one that should have the treasure. Eventually they will see your sailboat. They will assume the treasure is with you."

After a long pause, Molly's face registered the logic. "Right," she said. "But without a boat they can't follow us."

"They will panic. Maybe even race back to Santa Rosalia to hire a boat to search for you."

"Which will give us time to double back for the treasure," Molly said.

Digby studied Pancho, who held the guide rope in an outstretched hand, and said, "As much as I appreciate what you are doing for us, the treasure deserves to be in a museum."

"*Posible.*"

"We can announce the discovery together."

"I have no need for fame." He motioned toward the crown in Digby's hand. "If you survive, I will help you. But you must take the curse and leave."

"Hurry," Molly said, taking the rope from Pancho.

Digby removed Molly's backpack and placed the crown inside. He slung it across his shoulders and turned back to Pancho. "Protect the treasure until we return."

Pancho's turquoise eyes radiated kindness. *"Por supuesto."*

Digby glanced once more at the approaching cloud of dust, and then ducked into the dark tunnel of lava and followed Molly down the rope.

CHAPTER THIRTY-FOUR

Magdalena Bay, Baja California Sur

After a quick splashdown to retrieve Skegs and the blowgun from the dock in front of Cantina del Cielo, Fish was airborne again.

"Did you get someone at the camp?" Fish asked.

"Lalo. He's all set. Guy in the Range Rover pulled in just as we finished talking. Trap's been laid."

"Excellent."

"Tell me you're not planning to blow one of those darts into the guy from a moving airplane."

"And hit Lalo? Too risky."

"Sounds risky no matter how you do it."

"The plan is to fly to the other side of the island and take my panga back into the bay. That way you'll be able to pull directly up to them and see if Lalo needs help with the engine."

"*I'll* be pulling up to them? No way, Spartacus. I'm not some servant you can use as a shield. What if the dude throws one of those knives?"

"He knows what I look like."

"I'm starting not to like you very much."

"I'll be crouched between the panga seats. Under a tarp. We'll stick some fishing rods out to the side. He'll never suspect a person under there. As soon as you pull up, I'll dart him."

"And how long does it take for this poison to take effect?"

"Depends."

"On what?"

"On where I hit him."

CHAPTER THIRTY-FIVE

Long Beach, California

Toozie flew into Long Beach and took a cab to the Museum of Latin American Art, where she wandered the exhibits pretending to admire the sculptures and paintings and ancient masks. She'd dressed business casual for the occasion: jeans, boots, and a white stitched blouse beneath a denim jacket. She topped it off with a Toyo hand-braided cowboy hat. A man in a security guard uniform stood near the front desk, and she slowly worked her way toward him.

To the average art patron the guard appeared to be bored. To Toozie he looked sinister. He wore his black hair roached back and kept his face cleanly shaved. His eyes were dark, his skin tanning-booth brown. The uniform was freshly pressed, and he wore patent leather shoes that shined like polished tar. Toozie also recognized the X3 taser gun that hung from a belt fit snugly around his flat stomach. Toozie pegged him at midthirties. She also pegged him as a smoker.

"Excuse me," she said, approaching the front desk. He turned, and she saw his name tag. "Jim, I'm having a terrible nicotine fit. You wouldn't happen to have an extra cigarette?"

The security guard straightened and smiled. "I'm about to go on break. We can smoke in the parking lot."

"Great," Toozie said, her opal eyes flashing.

Harvey Dixon unclipped his walkie-talkie and relayed his cigarette break to someone who replied, "Five minutes."

Toozie watched him reclip the walkie-talkie and said, "They run a tight ship."

"Paranoid pricks," Harvey said. "The boss says I've got to give notice of my whereabouts whenever I leave the main floor." He shook his head without loosening a strand of hair. "You know how many cameras are in this place? Christ, the guy up in the booth knows where I am even before I do."

He opened the door and Toozie followed the security guard out to the parking lot.

"You worked here long?" she asked.

Harvey stopped at the edge of the sidewalk and shook two cigarettes loose from a pack. "Few months," he said and handed her a smoke.

"Had to arrest anyone yet?"

"Ran off some teenagers a few weeks ago. A loiterer every now and again. Mostly it's busywork. Watching school groups and retired folks pretend to give a shit. A few professors now and then." He reached into his pocket for a lighter and handed it to her.

"Here's the thing," Toozie said, ignoring the lighter. "I don't smoke."

"You said you were having a nicotine fit."

"I lied." She handed back the cigarette and the lighter. "You're okay with lying, Jim? Or is it, Harvey?"

Harvey Dixon fumbled with the lighter and dropped the cigarette to the sidewalk.

"Those cameras," Toozie said. "Are they on us now?"

"Of course," he said, regaining his composure. He bent down to retrieve the cigarette. "The whole place is covered."

"Then I suggest you light your cigarette and pretend like we know each other."

Harvey lit his cigarette. "It's going to look a little funny, me handing you a cigarette and you handing it back."

"Tell them I smoke a different brand."

"How did you know my name?"

"I know a lot of things."

"Like—?"

"Like you're an art thief, for starters."

Harvey sucked at the cigarette, eyeing her through the smoke. "You a cop?"

"Nope."

"The museum hire you?"

Toozie shook her head.

Harvey smiled. "An art collector, perhaps?"

"I like art."

"I'm out of the business."

"Where's Slim?"

"Who?"

"Did you enjoy your time at Lompoc?"

Harvey took a deep drag and watched as it slowly swirled from the corner of his tight mouth. "Who the hell are you?"

"As far as the camera knows, just a friend. As far as you're concerned, I'm the only thing standing between you and millions of dollars' worth of treasure. Now take out your cell phone and call your brother."

"And if I refuse?"

"You can say goodbye to Jim the security guard."

"You'd turn me in just like that?"

"Just like that."

Harvey dug into his pocket and removed his cell phone. He glared at her. "Black-market art collectors are a select group. I know the players. You're not one of them."

"The archaeologist better still be alive."

"You're a private eye?"

"Make the call."

"Why didn't you say so? I've got no beef with the archaeologist."

"So why's he missing?"

Harvey casually sucked at the cigarette. "How the hell should I know?"

"Is your brother armed?"

"Usually. But he's not after the archaeologist."

"The archaeologist and the treasure are one and the same as far as I'm concerned."

Harvey shrugged.

Toozie gestured toward the cell phone. "Call him and tell him any harm comes to the archaeologist, Jim the security guard goes back to prison."

"Slim won't give a shit. Barbie offered him thirty million for the treasure. Stump'll probably pay even more."

"Ronald Stump?"

"The one and only."

Toozie caught herself smiling. "Does this Barbie live in Cabo?"

"You could say that."

"Tell me about him."

Harvey blew a series of smoke rings into the air. "*Her.* The creepiest woman you'll ever meet. Even scares Slim, and that's saying something." He took an abbreviated lungful of smoke. "The only way Slim leaves your archaeologist alone is if Barbie says so. And the only way Barbie says so is if it involves large payments in cash."

"How do I meet this Barbie?"

Harvey smiled for the first time, and Toozie watched tendrils of smoke swirl out from the gaps in his teeth.

CHAPTER THIRTY-SIX

Magdalena Bay, Baja California Sur

After landing his seaplane and transferring to the panga, Fish hid beneath a canvas tarp between the middle thwarts. He and Skegs had piled lobster traps and old buoys beneath the tarp, leaving just enough space for Fish to crouch between the equipment and the gunwale. A cluster of fishing rods was also added, their tips jutting over the side. Fat trolling rods with final eyelets similar in size to the hollow end of the four-foot Indonesian blowgun. The blowgun rested on the gunwale, its barrel carefully loaded with a hollow-pointed dart swollen with poison.

Skegs stood at the stern, keeping the panga on an even plane across the flat bay. As he approached Lalo's panga dead in the water, he slowed. Lalo waved.

"Need help?" Skegs called out in Spanish. He stole a glance at the tattooed man at the bow. Snake Hissken looked impatient. And hot. Sweat beaded his scaly skin like leprosy.

"Sí," Lalo said. He turned and spoke to his customer in English.

Snake crossed himself and nodded reluctantly.

Moments later, as Skegs pulled to the stern of Lalo's panga, Fish peeked above the gunwale. Through the nest of fishing rods, he saw the hit man staring intently at Lalo and Skegs. The bowie knives were most likely hidden, but clearly visible at Snake's waist was a protrusion the size of a large pistol. Fish watched the annoyed bodyguard wipe sweat from the ridge of his black eye patch.

Fish adjusted the blowgun.

A body shot made a larger target area, but the pain of the poison entering the bloodstream would be far more effective with a shot to the face. Fish took a calming breath. The inner bay was flat as a coffin lid. Skegs and Lalo hovered motionless over the outboard, seemingly aware of the expatriate's decision to fire. Hissken, too, was statuelike, as if the lack of movement would keep him cool. A fortunate, albeit futile, miscalculation on the part of the lanky ex-wrestler.

Fish closed an eye, aimed, and exhaled in one fast, smooth motion, hearing a reassuring hollow sound emanate from the end of the blowgun. He watched his target flinch as the dart connected. Then the bodyguard rocketed to a standing position, clawing at his neck and screaming in tongues as Fish quickly reloaded the blowgun.

Snake Hissken plucked the dart from his neck and reached for his gun. Fish fired again, and then flung the tarp from his head and lunged for the outboard throttle. At the same moment, Skegs shoved Lalo overboard. The sudden movement knocked Snake off balance. He toppled over a bench seat and crashed to the floorboards, firing wildly. Bullets whizzed overhead. Fish felt a searing pain in his side and gunned the engine. He aimed for the panga, preparing to ram it at full speed, when Skegs frantically waved him off. Fish cut the engine. He turned sharply and allowed the boat to bang into the side of Lalo's panga.

Snake Hissken lay propped on his back between the thwarts, his arms limp at his sides. The gun was beneath him in a puddle of saltwater. His one eye stared blankly at the sky. His other eye, covered by the black patch, leaked blood around the edges. The patch glistened with wetness, and from its center protruded a three-inch steel dart, its hollow shaft embedded deeply into the bodyguard's eyeless socket.

The neurotoxins had entered Snake's bloodstream, quickly disarming his central nervous system. Fish sat, unsteady, and watched Skegs step into view. The mescal salesman reared back a leg and kicked Snake in the ribs.

"You shot at me, goddammit!"

Snake gave no reaction, and Skegs bent down and poked him in the face. "I know you're not dead. I can see your chest moving. Say something, asshole."

"He can't," Fish said.

"Why not?"

"His vocal chords are paralyzed."

"I say we dump him overboard. Do the world a favor."

"Bad idea."

"Can he hear us?"

"Most likely."

Skegs stared down at the paralyzed man. "You ever shoot at me again, *cabrón*, and I swear to God I'll do more than kick you in the ribs." He glanced over at Fish. "Hey, you alright?"

"Sure."

Fish stood and Skegs saw the crimson streak running down his pant leg.

"The hell you are." Skegs stepped over Snake's body and boarded the panga. "How bad is it?"

Fish removed his shirt and revealed a two-inch gash where the bullet had winged him. "Just a scratch."

"More like a furrow. You're gonna need stitches."

"No time. First-aid kit's in the plane."

Skegs frowned. "Man, when are you going to quit being so damn reckless? I knew this was a harebrained idea. You may have more money than God, but you're not immortal. No matter what that damn donkey of yours says."

"She's a mule," Fish said and gingerly stepped aboard Lalo's panga. He leaned over Snake's face and stared into his unblinking eye. "Listen carefully. My friend here would gladly toss you overboard, but I'm inclined to let you live. This vendetta of yours is futile. I suggest you follow that other tenet, live and let live. As for what happened in La Paz, saving you from my friend here makes us even. So now you're going to drive that Range Rover back to

Cabo and tell your boss to call off the hunt. We have the treasure. Game over."

Skegs grunted disapprovingly. "Didn't we just discuss your addiction to recklessness? This cat's bent on killing your sorry ass. You know he'll be back."

"Maybe."

"So we just let him go?"

"Yep."

"But the dude can't even blink."

"The poison wears off quickly."

"I'm not liking you right now."

Fish pressed his shirt into his wound to slow the bleeding. "Toss his gun. And check him for knives." Fish turned to Lalo, who'd crawled back aboard and stood at the stern, ashen-faced and dripping with saltwater. Fish reached into his pocket and removed a bundle of hundred-dollar bills.

"*Gracias, amigo*," he said and held out the payment.

Lalo waved him off. "No, señor," he said. In Spanish he added, "You are more a brother than a friend. Anytime you need help. No matter the risk."

"*Muchisimas gracias*," Fish replied. "I'd like this man returned to shore and sent on his way." He started to pocket the money when Skegs plucked it from his hand.

"Yeah, yeah, nice gesture and all, but don't be a dumbass, Lalo. We could have been killed. Take the money." He held it out.

Lalo didn't move.

"I'll hold it for you," Skegs said and pocketed the cash. Then he flung Snake's gun into the bay and patted him down for knives. "Hot damn," he whistled and unsheathed two blades strapped to Snake's ankles. "You weren't kidding."

"Time to fly," Fish said faintly and collapsed to the floor of Lalo's panga.

CHAPTER THIRTY-SEVEN

Cabo San Lucas, Baja California Sur

Ronald Stump used his dock key and descended the causeway where the less fortunate members of the Cabo San Lucas yacht club kept their boats. He stopped at the sixty-eight-foot Bertram, *King of Diamonds*, and stepped aboard unannounced. Charlie Diamond appeared on deck, a small hand gaff gripped tightly in his hand. He swayed slightly, his eyes glazed with drink.

"A bit paranoid, don't you think, Charlie? It's hardly past breakfast."

Charlie tossed the gaff to the fighting chair. "Jesus Christ. You know better than to come aboard someone's boat without permission."

"I thought we were friends."

"Yeah, BFFs," Charlie growled. "What the fuck do you want?"

Stump forced his smirk into a smile. "Barbie paid me a visit."

Charlie blinked his eyes into narrow slits. "Bullshit," he said, dragging a fat finger down a ruddy cheek.

"Listen, Charlie, if there's one thing you know about me it's that I don't like small talk. Barbie's playing you."

"Thanks for stopping by." Charlie turned for the salon.

"She says you were offered the Jesuit Treasure for twenty million."

Charlie halted abruptly. "Did she?" he slurred without turning around.

"There's more."

Charlie made a wobbly turn. "She launders money through her fucking topless joint. Big deal. That doesn't make her the boss of me."

"She mentioned a few indiscreet friends sent to steal your art. Seems they uncovered something less...artful."

"*Barbie* told you that?"

"She seemed almost excited."

"But—"

"There's more, of course."

Charlie's red face dropped. He peered over at the gangway, where a young couple in the throes of a hangover walked by discussing breakfast burritos.

"Let's talk somewhere more private," Charlie said and led Stump into the salon, where a blender half full of booze sat on the bar. "Bloody Mary?"

He glanced at his Rolex. "Maybe twelve hours from now."

Charlie topped off his cocktail.

"She wanted me to send my bodyguard over here to try and scare you off the treasure," Stump continued.

Charlie choked on a mouthful of tomato-spiked vodka. "Scare me off the treasure? Fuck that." He refilled his glass, and then glared at Stump. "Why *your* bodyguard? You two partnering up now?"

Stump gave the smallest grin Charlie had ever seen. "She's stirring the pot, Charlie."

"Screw that. I've always paid her asking price. Never double-crossed her. I even agreed to plaster half the goddamn city in pink billboards for half my usual price. Where's the loyalty?"

"She wants that crown."

"Who wouldn't?"

"She also wants you out of Cabo."

"I'm not leaving."

"She mentioned a hundred million for the rest of the treasure."

Charlie laughed. "The woman's delusional. No one's that stupid."

Stump was silent.

Charlie squinted to clear his vision. "You're planning to buy the whole fucking lot, aren't you? That's why you're here. Trying to play a fast one on Charlie Diamond. Well, it won't work."

"I'm not interested in the treasure. Not for that asking price."

"Maybe I'll steal it from her. You know, an eye for an eye."

Stump turned toward the salon door, and then turned back. "There is one more thing, Charlie."

Charlie glowered at the real estate tycoon.

"She called you an amateur."

Charlie slammed his cocktail glass to the bar, shattering it in his hand. He didn't even glance down. "And does she know you're here to do her bidding?"

"Of course not."

"And if I don't believe you?"

"Ask her yourself."

Charlie took a breath. Checked his hand. Finding it uncut, he swiped the broken glass from the bar to the floor and emptied the blender into a new glass. "Maybe I will. Let her know nobody fucks with Charlie Diamond."

"That's the spirit."

Charlie nodded fervently. "Demand my art back, and then some for the trouble."

"Turn the tables on the hairless turncoat."

"Damn straight."

"See you around," Stump said and exited the salon, a thin smile briefly stretching his immutable smirk.

CHAPTER THIRTY-EIGHT

Punta Baja, Baja California Sur

After loading Fish into the plane and dressing his wound, Skegs forced the expatriate to drink a second helping of water before allowing him to start up the engines.

"You pass out again and I'm calling this whole thing off."

"I didn't pass out, I got a little light-headed."

Skegs narrowed his gaze. "I'm not landing this plane for you."

"You won't have to," Fish assured him and lifted from the bay.

They gained altitude and crossed the peninsula, flying over the port town of Santa Rosalia before banking up the Baja coastline. As they approached Punta Baja, Fish spotted the familiar refurbished schooner sailing away from the rocky beach. The one he'd seen the day before tacking about offshore.

"That schooner was around here yesterday," he said to Skegs, who'd nodded off.

"That's nice," the mescal maker mumbled without opening his eyes.

"The *Taliswoman*."

"Uh-huh."

"Perfectly restored turn-of-the-century."

"Hmmm..."

"I'd like to meet the captain someday. See who's responsible for the fine workmanship."

Fish flew over the sailboat and had angled in low for a landing at Punta Baja when he spotted the convertible Cadillac parked above the stuck pickup.

"Uh-oh."

Skegs's eyes snapped open.

"That wasn't here yesterday." He pulled back on the yoke and the plane porpoised skyward.

Skegs grabbed the binoculars and scanned the hillside. "Turn!" He reached out and spun the plane's yoke away from shore. The plane veered sharply over the water, sending bales of hay from the makeshift paddock sliding across the back of the plane.

Fish grimaced in pain and regained control and turned to his friend. "What the hell was that for?"

"I don't like bullets."

"Someone was shooting at us?"

"From the entrance of that cave. A guy in a cowboy hat. He's got a couple of hostages tied up and sitting on the ground. All bandaged up. The cowboy was aiming a long-barreled pistol at us."

"First Snake, now Slim."

"Who?"

"Bounty hunter named Slim Dixon. Toozie mentioned him yesterday."

"Thanks for filling me in. Tell me again why I agreed to be your friend?"

"To learn how to catch snook?"

"That's not funny."

Fish circled south and set a course for the sailboat in the distance.

"You really think now's the time to discuss old boats?" Skegs asked. He trained the binoculars back at the hillside. "Our shooter's hightailing it down to his Caddy. Leaving the two injured dudes in the cave."

"Twin brothers who stole the treasure from Digby. Slim must have found them and came back to their hiding place. Only something's wrong."

"Yeah, like you not telling me about the twins either."

"I thought they'd be washed down the arroyo and drowned in that upside-down old truck. I was half expecting our archaeologist to be washed up with them." He closed in on the sailboat. "When we flew over the *Taliswoman* a few minutes ago, I saw a man standing next to the woman sailor. I'd like to have a little chat with those two. Find out why such interest in Punta Baja."

"Maybe they're honeymooners."

"Punta Baja's not your ideal romantic getaway."

"Could be scuba divers. Lots of rocks to explore."

"They'd dive the islands, not the shoreline."

"Maybe so."

"I think they have the treasure."

"You *what?*"

"Why else would Punta Baja be such an attraction?"

"The cowboy definitely didn't want us hanging around."

"If the treasure were up in that cave, he wouldn't be racing back to his car."

"It's on the boat. How the hell's he going to get it?"

"He's not." Fish buzzed low over the boat. "Grab a water jug from the back and pour it out."

"You've got to be kidding. Piss break? Now?"

Fish gave him a sideways glance. "Fill it with a couple of fishing weights." He reached across the dashboard and grabbed a pen and pad of paper from the airplane's glove compartment.

Minutes later they began circling the sailboat. Fish opened the pilot-side window and dropped the weighted jug with its handwritten note inside. The jug splashed into the sea a hundred feet off the Medusa maidenhead.

Fish flew ahead and landed. When he turned to taxi back toward the sailboat, he saw the man with the blond mustache snag the jug with a long-handled gaff. The man freed the note and waved.

Fish shut down the engines and deployed the inflatable dinghy. "Permission to come aboard?" he called out.

"Permission granted," Molly said.

Skegs pitched the dinghy's bow rope around the nearest stanchion and moments later he and Fish stood on the teakwood deck of the refurbished schooner. After quick introductions, Digby handed Fish back the note.

"The guy shot at your plane?" he asked.

Skegs nodded. "Tall cat in a ten-gallon hat."

"You know him?" Fish asked.

Digby shook his head.

"He left two injured guys tied up in a cave," Skegs added.

"Kidnappers."

"We dropped them at Santa Rosalia yesterday," Molly said. "They needed medical attention."

Fish waited for an explanation.

"Long story," Digby said. "Your note mentioned the private investigator, Toozie. You're working for her?"

"She's a friend," Fish answered, adjusting his mullet-skin cap to block the sun. "I was in the area so she asked me to look around. I spotted your truck stuck in the wash."

"The *chubasco* yesterday did a real number on us."

"Toozie said the museum curator is behind all of this."

"Stanley?"

"He hired the twins to follow you. Apparently, they went rogue once they had the treasure. That's when Slim got involved."

Digby's face darkened. "The cowboy?"

"Looks like it."

"Speaking of treasure," Skegs interrupted, his eyes drifting about the deck. "Where you hiding it?"

"We don't have it."

"*What*?" Fish said incredulously.

"The Indian took it while we were dropping off the twins at Santa Rosalia."

"Took it?" Fish asked.

"Indian?" Skegs added.

"We hid it in the cave. He must have been watching and took it while we were gone."

"That explains the cowboy's sudden flash of anger," Skegs said.

Digby nodded. "I'm sure he expected to find the treasure there. Tracked down the twins somehow and forced them to take him there."

Fish turned to Molly. "This is a hell of a boat. You do all the work yourself?"

Molly nodded.

"If you ever decide to sell—"

"She's not for sale."

"Back to this cowboy," Digby interjected. "If he thinks we have the treasure, he'll come after us."

"Which is why you need to be honest with us," Skegs said.

Fish added, "I have a vault. Well hidden. The treasure will be safe there."

"I told you, we don't have it."

"Right," Skegs said. "Some mysterious cave dweller walked off with it."

Digby and Molly exchanged looks.

Fish sighed. "It's been a trying day."

"Looks like it was more than trying," Molly said and motioned toward the fresh bloodstain marking Fish's waistline.

Fish glanced down and dabbed at the wetness with the back of his hand.

"Serves you right for making me close it with superglue and a butterfly bandage," Skegs spat.

Fish ignored the comment. "It's nothing," he said to Molly.

Molly didn't seem all that convinced, but let it be. "The cave dweller's name is Pancho," she said. "He lives in the lava tubes."

Skegs choked back a laugh. "While you were away a hermit steals millions from you, and when you show back up he waltzes down the mountain to introduce himself?"

"I'm not sure he really wants it," Molly said.

Skegs slapped his thigh. "The fun just keeps on rolling."

"It's true," Digby added.

Fish twisted the crimp holding his goatee and said, "You're telling us this hermit helped you get away?"

"Somehow he knew the cowboy was coming," Digby explained, then quickly added, "Not *the* cowboy, but someone up to no good. Pancho wanted to warn us."

"Warn you away from the treasure's more like it," Skegs blurted.

Digby said, "Pancho said the person coming would realize we took the treasure and come after us. The cowboy doesn't know about Pancho. Neither do the twins."

"Then the treasure is safe for now," Fish said. "But—"

"*We* aren't," Molly finished his thought.

"Especially not if you head toward Santa Rosalia. That's the closest town and his best bet for a boat."

Her shoulders slumped in resignation. "If he really does think we have the treasure, sooner or later he'll find us."

"Jesus," Digby complained. "It really *is* cursed."

"What's really cursed?" Skegs asked.

The archaeologist grabbed Molly's backpack and removed the crown-shaped whale bone decorated in black pearls.

"Holy shit!" Skegs exclaimed.

Fish gave a pained smile.

"Legend says the local Indians fashioned it from a sacred whale bone." Digby handed the crown to Skegs. "They wanted the Jesuits to get the hell out. It worked."

"Change of plans," Fish said.

Everyone stared at him.

"Digby, you and Molly turn around and sail back to Punta Baja. Anchor just offshore and take the dinghy to the north end of the bay and hide."

Molly shook her head. "I'm not leaving the *Taliswoman* unprotected. Not with that cowboy after us. Who knows what he'll do to her."

"You won't be leaving her unprotected," Fish said.

"You said leave her at anchor and hide."

"I'll be on board."

CHAPTER THIRTY-NINE

Cabo San Lucas, Baja California Sur

Charlie Diamond stumbled from his yacht and into downtown Cabo San Lucas. It was noon, and the tequila two-step was in full swing. Straw-hatted gringos jockeyed for position along the main road, gawking at Chihuahuas posing in tiny top hats. Crowds of college kids tossed pesos at dueling iguanas wearing brightly colored, lizard-size swim trunks. Time-share salesmen swirled through the crowds like unwanted smoke. Charlie ignored it all.

Barefoot children selling Chiclets tugged at his pockets as taxicabs blared horns and spit exhaust into the air. A Cessna airplane flew low overhead with a banner that read *Cabo Wabo Jello Shots Heal Sunburn.* Charlie gave an unsteady thumbs-up. Then he dropped a ten-peso coin to the sidewalk. The Chiclets children swarmed. He ducked unsteadily into Plaza de los Mariachis and stared longingly at the world's smallest bar. Slim's Elbow Room was bursting like a blister in the sun. Charlie longed to join the drunken tourists, but instead spilled back onto the sidewalk.

He ambled up Marina Boulevard and stopped at the entrance to the Giggling Marlin. Across the street, Plaza del Sol and its anchor tenant, the two-story Pink Octopus, beckoned. The Tickling Tentacles Day Spa offered full-body massages twenty-four hours a day. A *farmacia* on the ground floor advertised tequila-flavored love pops for $9.99. Dirigible-size posters over the windows displayed a smiling orange worm lounging inside an orange-tinted lollipop. The tail end of the worm curled provocatively upward.

The aroused annelid wore a sombrero with the word *Cialis* printed across the brim.

Charlie waited for a long line of ATVs to pass through the intersection, and then stumbled across the street and into the strip club. The cold air and loud music sobered him briefly. He blinked until his eyes adjusted to the smoky gloom, straining to see the figure gyrating on the stage. The sight briefly distracted him. Until the music stopped and the nude dancer retreated into the shadows. Charlie hurried to the bar and ordered a Cape Cod. A topless bartender poured him two.

"Midday special, handsome," she said with rehearsed lustiness. "That'll be twenty bucks."

"Twenty bucks?" Charlie slurred. "What kind of special is that?" He slammed a twenty to the bar. "Barbie's worse than Jessie James. At least that outlaw used a gun to rob people."

"Please keep your voice down," the bartender said, using her bust to slide the two drinks forward. "If the doorman hears you there could be trouble." She wiggled the drinks free without spilling a drop. "You do realize that stress is the number one killer of middle-aged men? Lucky for you I'm working the massage table in an hour."

"Some other time," Charlie said, and downed the first Cape Cod. "Tell Barbie her friend Charlie Diamond is here."

The bartender plucked the twenty from the bar. "She doesn't come down to the floor."

A flash of sunlight caught Charlie's attention and he turned to see two overweight men in *What Happens in Cabo Stays in Cabo* T-shirts enter the club. They high-fived each other and walked to the far end of the bar, where the bartender suddenly reappeared.

"Suckers," Charlie mumbled.

A Lynyrd Skynyrd tune turned Charlie's attention toward the stage, where a buxom woman with a uniquely tattooed chest gyrated around a pole. Charlie stood with his remaining drink and joined the men crowding the stage. He eyeballed the artwork covering the dancer's chest. Both enormous breasts were tattooed to resemble matching margarita glasses, each with a lime-colored nipple. Beneath each bulbous cocktail glass was a matching stem running the length of her torso and disappearing into a thong.

"You like Las Margaritas?" came a sultry voice into Charlie's ear. He jerked sideways and fell into one of the few unoccupied tables, spilling his glass of vodka and cranberry juice. "Careful," the voice said. "Booze we can replace. A handsome man like you, not so much."

"You startled me," Charlie huffed, his anger ebbing at the sight of the raven-haired woman. She bore a striking resemblance to the topless bartender.

"Octopussy," the woman introduced herself and held out a hand tipped with fluorescent pink nails.

"Like the James Bond movie?"

"Like the manager of Tailfish Charters."

"Tailfish Charters?" A new drink suddenly appeared and Charlie happily accepted it.

"You fish, right?"

"Um?"

She traced a pink nail down his arm. "For two thousand bucks you can troll all afternoon with Las Margaritas helping to bait your hook. All of our yachts are state-of-the-art. Drinks are free."

"Troll?"

"Marlin, dorado, tuna." She winked. "Or what we like to call 'the other pink meat.'" She let her finger linger on Charlie's hip.

"That's a lot of money."

"It's a very special charter."

"Cabo's been fished out."

"Which is why a full-body massage is included in the price."

"Two thousand bucks for a rubdown?"

"A very special rubdown."

"Jesus Christ!" he barked, suddenly remembering why he was there.

"Please, sir. The doorman—"

"Yeah, the fucking doorman. Tell him Charlie Diamond is here to see Barbie." He turned his attention back to the stage.

"I'm very sorry."

"Whatever," Charlie replied without taking his eyes off the stage.

"You should look at a woman when she talks to you," came a gruff voice.

Charlie turned and stared into the largest fist he'd ever seen.

When he awoke, Charlie was slumped in a glass chamber the size of a telephone booth. He had been stripped of his clothes and his hands and feet were secured with plastic flex cuffs. A strong chemical odor filled his nostrils.

"Hello Charles," came a familiar trill from speakers in the ceiling.

Charlie blinked into the bright lights. "Where the fuck am I?"

"Disparaging my club and cursing at my bartender. Tsk, tsk. That was quite reckless."

Charlie yanked at his restraints. "Let me go! You set me up, goddamn you! You took all of my artwork. Now you think you can blackmail me?"

A sudden spray misted the chamber. Charlie coughed violently and felt his skin begin to burn.

"It's no use, Charles. You cannot leave until we are done with you."

"*We*?"

"My friends have decided that you need a good scrubbing. Think of it as a day at the spa."

"What friends? You don't have any fucking friends."

The spraying mechanism stopped and the lights dimmed. The mist settled on Charlie's skin like damp cellophane. He glanced down in horror as the hair on his arms and legs began to dissolve.

"Look around, Charles. The audience is applauding."

Charlie blinked through the fog of a broken nose and wet glass, and saw a horde of mannequins.

"You're fucking sick!" Charlie shouted.

"I think you have it backward, Charles. I feel quite well. As I think you will, now that you've been treated. Even better when you wake up without all of that nasty hair."

"What do you mean wake up? I am awake, goddamn it!"

"You can thank me later."

"I can have you arrested. Blackmailing and stealing is a crime, even in Mexico." He swiveled his neck in alarm as his hair began to melt. "This shit burns. What the hell is it? Where are you! Let me go or I'll expose your black-market business. Your secret infatuation with dolls. Your—"

Charlie heard the sprayers engage and saw a fresh cloud of vapor descending. He yanked at his binds and kicked at the glass walls.

"Let me out of here!" he screamed, then gasped for breath.

Barbie blew him a kiss.

"Nighty night, Charlie boy," vectored through his mind as unconsciousness enveloped him like a crypt.

CHAPTER FORTY

Santa Rosalia, Baja California Sur

Slim Dixon had expected the treasure to be in the cave where the twins left it. Instead, he found a cavern of dirt. He'd been contemplating shooting the brothers for double-crossing him when the low-flying seaplane banked into the bay intending to land. Wary of visitors, Slim fired a warning shot and then watched with fascination as the plane landed near a sailboat he hadn't seen before. A sailboat—recognized by the twins as carrying the archaeologist—and most likely the missing treasure.

Slim left the twins tied up in the cave and sprinted down the dirt path to his car. He drove recklessly up the arroyo and through the canyon, squealing onto Highway 1. He raced into Santa Rosalia and skidded into the parking lot at the old marina, where he hoped to hire a fishing boat to take him out to sea. Pay the captain a few extra pesos *not* to fish. Set the throttle at full speed and not stop until they'd found the sailboat with the archaeologist and the loot. Unravel the mystery of the seaplane. Take hostages if barter was required. Or better yet, dispose of the bodies at sea. Transfer the treasure to the dinghy and light the rest on fire. Sailboat, seaplane, chartered fishing boat. None of it mattered to Slim. Not once he'd secured the treasure.

"Live and let die," Slim muttered as he tucked his gun into his waistband and hurried down the graveled lot to the short boat ramp. The sun was high overhead, and the first breeze of the day rocked the riggings of a half-dozen sailboats in various states of disrepair. Broken masts, torn sails, rusted scuppers, and all of them tucked into unkempt slips.

Slim searched for a charter fishing boat or a super panga, but saw only the broken-down rag boats. That and a plethora of tired-looking pelicans floating among piles of trash. No locals confronted him with offers of cartoon shirts or chili mangoes. No kids selling Chiclets or teenagers trafficking *mota*. Not even the ever-present *pangeros* offering half-day fishing or snorkel trips to the islands. No one, it seemed, wanted to engage the punishing sun.

Slim was hustling down the dock when a movement caught his eye. He turned and saw an old gringo with deep-set wrinkles and a bird's-nest beard emerge from the belly of a listing yawl. Slim hailed him. The man weaved a drunken course across the boat's peeling back deck and stepped to the dock.

"I'm looking to charter something," Slim said.

The old man flashed a toothless grin. "Wrong dock. Not that it matters much. Fishing boats left early this morning."

"Maybe a panga then. Something that floats. And runs fast."

"Fast?" He choked out a laugh and spat into the water. "Mister, fast left this place a long time ago."

"Five hundred. Cash."

The man squinted under the sunlight and inspected Slim more closely. "You ain't looking to fish in a getup like that." His gaze dropped to the hit man's alligator boots. "You Texan?"

Slim didn't answer. He reset his cowboy hat and felt his eyes go flat. He reached toward his waistband.

The old man drew back. "Five hundred, huh?" he said, suddenly sounding more sober than his eyes suggested. "First things first. I got a cooler of beer down below. You're welcome to it. Might take the edge off of this goddamn heat. Help you slide into Baja time."

"Some other time," Slim said, stepping toward the rusting boat. "You got an engine on this bucket of shit?"

The man flinched at the insult. He stumbled backward, and Slim reached out for the broken railing.

"Actually," the old man stammered. "You might have some luck down at the far end of the dock. Owner used to be a hell of a captain. Ran into a bit of trouble. Working it off for a year or two in the local hoosegow." The old man glanced around at nothing, and then lowered his eyes. "He ain't coming back for it. Not anytime soon."

"Keys?"

"I done led you to water. The drinking's up to you." He disappeared so suddenly below deck that Slim wondered if it had all been a mirage.

A seagull wheeled overhead, and Slim headed down the dock. He walked purposefully toward the far end, hardly noticing the great blue heron half asleep there in the sun. The giant bird squawked, beating its wings into a clumsy takeoff. Slim jerked back with a start and reached for his pistol, then spotted the guano-splattered fishing boat floating in the final slip. A twenty-six-foot sportfisher with a torn blue bimini flapping in the breeze and kicking up dust from a faded and cracked deck. The gunwales were coated in grime, the stainless-steel railings layered in salt. A broken lawn chair lay on its side among a pile of discarded fishing line. The name on the stern read: *Con Limón*, a faded lime wedge forming the accent above the *o*.

Slim stepped aboard. He peered though the clouded windows and saw a disheveled cabin. He knocked, waited, and knocked again. Silence. He walked to the bow and knelt by the front windows. He called out. Nothing. He returned to the deck and flung the broken lawn chair overboard and into the marina. He didn't know much about boats, but he knew a great deal about cars. He'd hot-wired dozens over the years. Diesels mostly. Trucks and old foreign collectibles. Side jobs. Small stuff to fill the void between the preferred carnage of contract work. All it took was something metallic to conduct the current. Connect the terminals on the solenoid and voilà. Pistons firing and exhaust flowing.

Slim rooted around the deck unsuccessfully for a piece of metal, and then hustled back to the Cadillac. He popped the trunk, grabbed the tire jack and a handful of rags, and returned to the *Con Limón*, pausing briefly at the old man's sailboat. See if he emerged again. Maybe remind the drunkard of the salutary value of anonymity. But the yawl's deck remained devoid of life. A sign of the man's longevity, Slim thought, as he hurried past the sailboat.

He boarded the *Con Limón* and raised the hinged engine cover, securing it to the back railing. He removed his cowboy hat, and moments later lay facedown inside the cramped engine compartment. He quickly found the solenoid, wrapped the handle of the jack with rags, and laid the tool across the terminals.

Sparks flew and the engine coughed to life. Black smoke billowed from beneath the stern. Slim pushed to his knees and looked around. The sun bore through the torn bimini like a butcher's knife, and other than the drowsy pelicans and a few seagulls, the dock was deserted.

Slim snatched his hat from the deck and quickly reset the engine cover. He climbed the open helm and stood on a soot-covered flybridge. The bubble compass was clouded with neglect, and the stainless-steel steering wheel was dull and pinged with salt.

Slim sat on the cracked bench seat, glanced around one more time, and jammed the throttle forward. The boat lurched and stopped. Slim gunned the engine again and a loud splintering sound filled the air, sending a cleat soaring across the bow. A second crack sent another cleat whizzing overhead, both trailing thick lengths of dock line.

Slim ducked, expecting more flying hardware, and felt the hull scrape against a cement dock piling. The boat careened off the end of the dock and Slim spun the wheel. He aimed for the mouth of the marina, mindless of the no-wake rule, and sped ahead at full speed, scattering pelicans and nearly running down a lone cormorant surfacing for air.

As he zoomed into the open ocean, a grin spread across his face. The treasure was on the horizon. Hidden beneath the hull of a sluggish sailboat. A boat captained by a lone female and an archaeologist. A deckhand with no more sea sense than a land tortoise.

Two against one.

An unarmed couple against an armed and deadly cowboy.

Slim liked the odds.

CHAPTER FORTY-ONE

Cabo San Lucas, Baja California Sur

Toozie caught the last morning flight to Cabo San Lucas and, by late afternoon, was standing on Marina Boulevard staring at a two-story shopping center with a huge mural of a pole-dancing pink octopus. Clutches of drunken tourists sang "La Bamba" from a tiny bar down the street. Taxicabs and rental cars clogged the intersection, horns blaring fruitlessly.

Cater-corner to the topless bar, a man in an enormous sombrero stood in front of the Giggling Marlin, offering five-dollar photos of his dancing iguana. A bevy of fraternity brothers whooped and hollered as the iguana bobbed its head to the rhythm of "Macarena" reverberating from a boom box. The song ended, and the college boys rushed across the street where Toozie stood waiting at the corner.

"Tits up!" one of the young men yelled as the group chugged cans of Tecate en masse. They tossed the twelve-pack of cans to the gutter and belched as one.

Toozie was about to comment on the charms of the male libido when a traffic cop suddenly appeared from beneath a shade awning across the street. The uniformed woman fearlessly entered the tidal wave of traffic. She blew hard on a whistle. Drivers reluctantly stopped. The traffic cop waved Toozie and her male entourage across. The boys raced inside the club, leaving Toozie outside to gape at the windows of a popular *farmacia*.

Huge posters advertised happy orange-colored worms. Above the pharmacy, a day spa offered twenty-four-hour massages. The special this month was a fifty-dollar, ten-minute minimassage guaranteed to relieve more than sunburn. A line of paunchy middle-aged men stood out front sucking on orange lollipops.

Toozie sighed and entered the club. Dance music blared from a brightly lit stage where two nude women gyrated around a ten-foot pole. The stage was crowded with the outstretched arms of the fraternity boys fanning hundred-peso notes through the air. Toozie felt nauseous.

It had been nearly twenty years since she'd fished Cabo's prolific blue waters, wandered its quaint cobblestone streets, imbibed its margaritas on unmolested beaches. It may have been a third-world country back then, but the eighteen-year-old aspiring private investigator felt safe traveling alone among its citizenry. Even late at night. Now, amid its glut of betting parlors and strip clubs and spring break bars, she mourned the death of Cabo's carefree charm. The sanctuary at the southern tip of Baja California had become a debauched cesspool.

"Can I help you?" came a surly voice behind her.

Toozie jumped. A man with a cinder-block head trimmed in spikes of blond hair stared down at her. He wore a tight-fitting suit and a smile befitting a hammerhead shark. Muscles rose like mountain ranges from his shoulders. He wore diamond studs in both ears and a kilo of gold around his neck. He leered at her through cold, catfish eyes.

"I'd like to see Barbie."

"She doesn't meet with patrons." He glanced down and scowled at her rough-hewn boots.

"I'm not a patron."

The man's neck twitched and Toozie wondered if that was a shrug.

"Then maybe you could deliver a message. It's urgent."

"I'm not Barbie's errand boy."

"You'll be an unemployed errand boy if your boss misses out on the Jesuit Treasure." Toozie watched the bouncer's fish eyes come to life. "That-a-boy," she said.

He scanned her body. "Where?"

"Safely guarded elsewhere."

His eyes returned to their dull state. "What if I say you're a liar?"

"I'd say you're far dumber than you look."

She held his gaze until he looked away.

"Tell Barbie I also know about the con. The hit man named Slim and his brother Harvey. And tell her I spoke with Ronald Stump. No one sees an ounce of treasure without my blessing."

"Is that some kind of threat?"

"Hey, I think you're catching on."

This time the massive shoulders flexed, and Toozie wondered if his suit coat would survive.

"Wait here," he said and lumbered past the stage, ignoring the nude girls and the boys waving pesos. He keyed in a combination, swung open a mirrored door, and turned sideways to squeeze through the opening. The door swung shut, and seconds later Toozie felt a tap on her arm. She turned and stared into a set of cat's eyes belonging to a woman in a business suit.

"You're late," she said.

"Say again?"

"The interview," she said grimly. "Jesus, are those cowboy boots?"

"Inappropriate?" Toozie asked, eyeing the weaponry at the businesswoman's belt. A stun gun similar to Harvey Dixon's hung beside a pair of gold handcuffs cinched to the woman's waist.

"Barbie's not going to like them."

"Barbie?" she feigned ignorance.

"The owner, of course."

"Of course," Toozie said, and followed the woman to the mirrored door.

CHAPTER FORTY-TWO

Punta Baja, Baja California Sur

From the water, the coastline north of Santa Rosalia was as bleak as anything Slim had ever seen. Bare rock, cobblestone beaches, craggy cliffs, everything a dirty, broken-down brown. Cacti as gaunt and lifeless as the cows that littered Highway 1. Slim stood at the helm of the stolen fishing boat and removed his cowboy hat, wiping sweat from his brow with the back of his hand. He squinted at a lone frigate bird high in the sky, its haunting black wings a fitting backdrop to the emptiness that surrounded him.

He replaced the hat and cursed. He'd expected the sailboat to be heading toward him, its deck loaded with treasure, its unlikely couple fleeing Punta Baja for the safety of Santa Rosalia. The seaplane, too, should have appeared overhead, possibly ferrying the treasure by air. In which case, Slim would gladly take the boaters hostage. Use their sailboat for target practice until they gave up the pilot and his destination.

But the ocean was a wasteland, and the sky a maddening reflection of his desperate isolation. The boat must have doubled back, or worse, been left adrift when its passengers boarded the seaplane with their priceless cargo. If they really had it in the first place. Someone would have to pay for this wild goose chase, and Slim knew just who it would be. The twins sent him out to the empty cave. Pretended to be surprised by the missing treasure. If the treasure was ever there at all. They would try to explain their double-cross, and Slim would make them pay. That he was looking forward to.

As he approached the bend of coastline leading to Punta Baja, he wondered if the twins had escaped their restraints. Pondered how far he would have to track them. They were injured and without water, and he knew it wouldn't take long. He was imagining which brother to kill first when he spotted the outline of the sailboat in the shallows near shore. The white mast was nearly hidden by the guano-covered bluffs, but the dark hull was easily recognizable. The boat was tucked close to the rocks. As Slim approached he studied the unusual bow maiden. He'd only caught a glimpse of it before. From the cave where he'd fired the warning shot. An enormous figurehead with locks of wooden hair flowing toward the waterline. Her wretched countenance transformed, her dark eyes bright and alive. A demigoddess restrained.

Medusa with a smile.

Slim freed the gun from his waistband. It made no sense for the couple to return here. Surely they'd seen him earlier. Watched as he led the twins to the cave. Heard the report of his warning shot across the sea. Why else would they have sailed away? Unless...

Slim kicked a boot angrily through the flimsy fiberglass helm. The archaeologist must have returned for the treasure. Hidden not in the cave, but somewhere closer to shore. Somewhere within easy loading distance. Probably transferred it and the double-crossing twins into the seaplane while he was foolishly racing to Santa Rosalia.

Slim scanned the shoreline for signs of life. The sun had mercifully dropped behind the mountain peak, and the Palo Verde and mesquite trees were deep in shadow. As he neared the abandoned sailboat, he wondered what valuables might be aboard. Surely there was a safe of some sort, jewelry, cash hidden in a drawer. Slim may have temporarily lost their trail, but he'd make the best of it. Ransack the ship and then sink it with a back-deck bonfire.

He slowed the powerboat and studied the waterline for movement. He doubted they'd set a trap. Not after he'd fired his gun. It would be suicide to lie in wait for a man of his talents. Still, he took his time. Longevity in his line of work took patience. Slim took a wide arc around the bow, watching for signs of life.

Nothing.

He loosened his cowboy hat and noticed the sailboat bobbing arrhythmically against the wake of the circling powerboat. He slowed to neutral, a nascent grin broadening his thin face. Maybe he'd been wrong about the seaplane. Maybe the pilot wasn't in on the treasure hunt. Maybe he'd only checked on the sailor and the archaeologist. To assure himself of their safety before flying off to wherever he'd been going before Slim airmailed his lead-filled warning.

Maybe the sailor and the archaeologist were still on board. Not expecting him to return so soon. Hiding when they heard the boat engine approaching. Spotting him through binoculars. No time to retrieve the treasure or free the truck from the arroyo. Slim had them dead to rights.

He raised the pistol. An osprey trilled overhead. Slim edged in closer and fired three rounds into the hull halfway between the waterline and deck. One at the stern, one at the fo'c'sle, and another near the bow. He waited for movement. Listened for a scream. Instead, he heard only the lapping of small waves against the shoreline.

He gunned the engine and rammed the sailboat's portside gunwale. Nothing. He reversed, circled the boat and rammed the starboard gunwale. Still nothing. He fired a round through the port windows, and then pulled the throttle to neutral. He waited, listening, watching the water for signs of movement.

Dead calm.

Something was wrong. The odds against hitting both occupants with blind shots were considerable. He sidled up to the maidenhead and stepped from the helm of the powerboat to Medusa's head, pausing briefly to tie the two boats together with an extra bowline. He turned and surveyed the arroyo and the cliff. In case he was being watched from shore. Nothing. He shuttled quickly down the sailboat's gunwale to the back deck, half expecting to see treasure strewn across the teak. Disappointment clouded his face.

He raised the deck hatch and stepped to the top of the stateroom ladder. He exhaled, and in one quick movement ducked inside and fired blindly into the salon. In case someone was stupid enough to surprise him.

"Surprise, surprise!" he called out, his eyes slowly adjusting to the gloom. He took another step down and fired again. "Guess who!"

Nothing.

He swept the barrel of the gun across the room and walked forward down the ladder. As his boots touched the floor, he spotted a silver crown covered in black pearls. It sat centerpiece on a teakwood coffee table. He lowered the gun.

He stepped toward the crown when an icy dread pricked the back of his neck. He began to turn when he realized his mistake. It came in the form of a steel shaft, its razor-sharp tip fitted with matching inch-long barbs. The spear entered the nape of his neck and exited his windpipe, splitting his Adam's apple like a fleshy deck of cards. The hit man toppled forward, momentarily driving the spear tip into the floorboards before rolling into a pool of blood, the pistol clattering harmlessly beneath the coffee table.

Fish stepped from the crawl space behind the ladder, his arm bleeding from a ricocheted bullet. He walked to the table and lifted the crown, glancing briefly at Slim, who lay gurgling through his torn throat.

"Some say this crown is cursed. I'm beginning to think they're right."

Fish looked up at the sound of his seaplane taxiing across the bay. When he glanced back down, Slim's eyes had glazed and the gurgling sound had ebbed into a single crimson bubble.

CHAPTER FORTY-THREE

Cabo San Lucas, Baja California Sur

The woman in the suit with the stun gun and the handcuffs led Toozie through a labyrinth of hallways to an upstairs room that housed a glassed-in stage and a single bright spotlight. The stage was an exact replica of the one below, with a stripper pole and chairs for a private audience. This stage, however, featured a mannequin with breasts painted to resemble margarita glasses. The audience was also made up of topless female mannequins, two of which were eerily similar to the naked pole dancers Toozie had seen earlier wowing the drunken college boys. Most troubling, however, was the bald man sat slumped in the front row, his arms tied to his sides, a sash securing him to the backrest of a chair.

"Remove your clothes," the suit told Toozie, and motioned her toward the stage. "Barbie's coming."

"Actually," Toozie said, turning toward the woman, "I'm not—"

She stopped at the sight of a lanky man in a muscle shirt entering the room. His long arms were covered in snake tattoos. He glared at her through a solitary orb. The other was hidden by a black patch. The man slithered beside the suit like a malediction— and appeared to cross himself.

No, didn't just *appear to. Did* cross himself.

Toozie was attempting, without much success, to make sense of this when she heard a noise and watched through the glass as a woman bearing a striking resemblance to the mannequins strutted into view.

"We know who you are," Barbie said, her voice tinny through the ceiling speakers. She puffed at a smokeless cigarette. "Or rather, who you are *not*. Prospective dancers rarely offer me insight into priceless treasure."

"Call off your man Slim."

"Slim?"

"Dixon," Toozie added when her cell phone vibrated. She reached for it and felt a powerful hand stop her. "Unless you want it broken, I suggest you unhand me," she said to the man with the eye patch.

Barbie nodded and Snake Hissken allowed Toozie to free the phone from her pocket.

"Put it on speaker," Barbie said.

The man's ropelike fingers reached for the phone. Toozie batted them away. "That's your last warning," she said and pressed the speaker button. "Toozie McGill."

"We found the archaeologist," came the voice of Atticus Fish, muffled slightly by the hum of propellers in the background.

"Alive or dead?" Toozie asked.

"Alive."

"I may be in trouble—"

Snake wrapped a hand around Toozie's face and spun her toward the woman in the suit, who aimed a taser at her midsection. Toozie wondered if it was coincidence that Harvey Dixon carried the same model back in Long Beach. The suit placed a finger to her lips with an admonishing shake of the head. Toozie nodded.

Snake slowly lifted his hand and Toozie yelled, "The Pink Octopus. Hurry Atticus!"

Snake snatched the cell phone from her hand. Two electrically charged darts pierced Toozie's white blouse and lodged in her rib cage. She fell to the floor in a spasm of pain.

"Toozie?" Fish called out.

"Indisposed at the moment," Barbie trilled.

"Who the hell are you?"

"Atticus is a rather unusual name," Barbie continued, exhaling a mouthful of invisible smoke. "Is it Greek?"

When Fish did not respond, Barbie said, "Your girlfriend stopped by to offer me advice. Odd, don't you think, Atticus?"

Toozie struggled to her knees, glaring at the woman with the stun gun. The woman had reloaded and was aiming it menacingly. Barbie made a motion and the woman lowered the gun.

"Toozie, please say something to Atticus so he knows you're still with us."

"Take care of Digby. I'll be fine."

"Sounds far from fine," Fish answered.

Barbie puffed at the plastic filter. "Tell us more about this Digby. Does he have my merchandise or has it been confiscated?"

"Digby is none of your business," Toozie growled.

The suit raised the stun gun.

"Now, now," Barbie crooned. "No need for that."

"The treasure is safe," Fish said. "The cowboy, however, is not."

"I'd like to leave now," Toozie said, and yanked the darts from her side. She flung them toward her assailant.

"I'm afraid," Barbie warbled, "that things have gotten more complicated than that."

"Bullshit. You heard Atticus. Game's over."

Barbie chortled softly. "You mentioned Slim? How 'not safe' is he, Atticus?"

"Infinitely."

"And my merchandise? You mentioned it was safe. Where is it exactly?"

"I believe you mean the Jesuit Treasure."

"Do not be coy."

"I'm hanging up," Atticus said. "And if I don't get a follow-up phone call from Toozie in the next five minutes telling me she is safe and on her way to meet me, you and I will have a very personal heart-to-heart. Very personal and very unpleasant."

"Threats will get you nowhere," Barbie said.

"Then consider it a proclamation."

"Here's my predicament, Atticus. The archaeologist has something of value that the very powerful covet. Powerful and dangerous. I'm offering you and your pretty friend a way out. The archaeologist, too."

"Four minutes and counting."

Barbie made a clicking sound with her tongue. "Atticus, you most certainly are in no position to bargain. Not if you want to see Toozie again."

"You're offering Toozie in exchange for the treasure?"

"Bravo," Barbie said. She motioned with her fingers, and Snake smothered Toozie's nose and mouth with a cloth.

"Toozie?" Fish called out.

"You've got twenty-four hours, Atticus," Barbie hissed. "And a word of caution before you decide to make good on your *proclamation* and try to play hero. Toozie's already being taken away. Soon she'll be far from Cabo. You will not find her unless I want you to. And if you're thinking about involving the police, you should know they are some of my most loyal customers."

Fish did not respond.

"Oh, and Atticus?" she cooed.

"Yes," he said sharply.

"The merchandise is to be delivered to my new yacht. Parked on the A Dock, just down the street. It's a nifty little sixty-eight-footer named the *King of Diamonds*. My bodyguard will be aboard. Once he confirms delivery, I will release your friend. Unharmed, course."

"It would be helpful if I knew your name."

"How rude of me," the club owner said. "Most people call me Barbie."

"Like the doll or the drug dealer?"

"Both."

CHAPTER FORTY-FOUR

Santa Rosalia, Baja California Sur

Fish unplugged the headset and placed the phone to the plane's center console. He carefully reglued his waist wound and changed the bandage, then checked his shoulder, which had finally stopped bleeding. He glanced at Skegs, who was listening to an iPod, unaware of the threats to Toozie. The mescal salesman sat in the copilot seat bobbing his head and inspecting the crown of black pearls. He'd taken the bone carving at Digby's insistence less than an hour earlier. The archaeologist had become superstitious as of late. Skegs gladly agreed to keep it safe.

Before leaving, they'd dumped Slim's body overboard and helped clean the sailboat of his blood. They also towed the stolen powerboat a mile out to sea, by seaplane, and left her adrift before flying toward Santa Rosalia to load up on supplies. The plan was to inform the local authorities about the abandoned fishing boat, and then return to Punta Baja to join Digby and Molly in their search for the hermit and the missing treasure.

Fish's recent discussion with Barbie, however, altered everything. He banked away from Santa Rosalia and headed due south toward Cabo San Lucas.

"Santa Rosalia's that way," Skegs said, removing his headphones and pointing toward the coastline.

"Toozie's in trouble."

"What?"

"Kidnapped."

Skegs set the crown to the dashboard. "Where?"

"Cabo."

"Someone nabbed her in Cabo?"

"Ever heard of the Pink Octopus?"

"Toozie was at a topless joint?"

Fish squinted with annoyance. "Shaking down someone named Barbie."

"Jesus, man. You're like a bull in a booby-trapped china shop. Shot twice and now you've got your sights set on Barbie. I don't like where this is going."

"Who is she?"

"A creepy android who owns the place. Buys a shitload of my cheapest mescal. Never seen her in person, though. Some kind of whacked-out germaphobe. Doesn't like to leave her lair. She's involved in this?"

"She wants the treasure."

"Toozie doesn't have it."

"Barbie thinks I do."

Skegs bored his eyes into Fish's profile. "And why the hell would she think that?"

"I might have inferred it."

"Of course you did."

"And the man we dumped overboard…?"

"Uh-oh."

"He worked for her. She knows all about the archaeologist, too. She said she'll release Toozie as soon as we deliver the treasure."

Skegs slid the crown toward Fish. "This is turning out to be the worst day of my life."

"I'm the one bleeding."

"Hate to say it, Hannibal, but you asked for it."

Fish said nothing.

"Don't go all high-and-mighty on me."

"I'd rather none of it happened."

"Come on, man. You went all postal on everyone. Popping a one-eyed freak with a blowgun. In the dude's empty eye socket.

That was off the fucking charts. Then you hide in a sailboat as bait. What did you think would happen?"

"Guess I didn't," he said resignedly. "Think, I mean."

Skegs sighed. "I could have stopped you, but I didn't. Guess I'm as crazy as you are."

Fish nodded. "Glad you're my wingman."

Skegs's face brightened. "I almost forgot." He raised the cell phone they'd taken off Slim's body before dumping him overboard. "While you were on the phone with Toozie, I checked the dead guy's calls."

"And?"

"A lot of blocked numbers."

Fish waited.

"Except one that kept coming up by name."

"Barbie?"

"Stump."

"Ronald Stump?"

"Is there any other?"

"I gave him a million cash."

"You what?"

"To stay away from Mag Bay."

Skegs whistled. "Hell, I'd stay away for half that."

"He's a developer."

"*I* like to build things."

"How many calls were there?"

"Half a dozen. Twice this morning. Last night. Yesterday morning. Seems they had a lot to talk about."

Fish's hand went to his goatee.

Skegs continued, "The one-eyed Snake dude trying to get to your island this morning? Maybe it was more than a personal grudge."

"Stump's a money guy. Greed gasses his tank. I'm nothing but a novelty to him."

"A novelty whose mule took a shit on his yacht. Who clocked his bodyguard. *And* told one of the richest dudes on the planet to stay the hell out of Mag Bay. Come on, man. You didn't do anything like that to me today and I was tempted to kill you a couple of times."

"I bought you breakfast."

"And so you live to annoy another day."

"Call Stump back."

Skegs scrolled down and hit redial. As it rang, he handed the phone to Fish.

Over the whine of the twin engines Fish heard the real estate mogul say, "Took you long enough. Did you kill those idiots and get my goddamned treasure?"

"I'm coming back for my million bucks. You set me up, but it backfired." The receiver was silent and Fish added, "I don't like bullies."

"Where's Slim?"

"Davy's Locker."

"You killed Slim?"

"Like I said, I don't like bullies."

"Where's the treasure?"

"I'm getting tired of your games, Stump. Snake's lucky to be alive. Did he deliver my message?" After a long moment of silence, Fish said, "I'll take that as a yes. Let's talk about Barbie."

"Who?"

"She's in Cabo. You're in Cabo. Sounds like a match made in heaven."

"You do not want to fuck with me, Fish."

"If you want the treasure, you'll call Barbie and tell her to meet you on your yacht. *Tonight.* Tell her *you* have the treasure."

"Why should she believe me?"

"Because you'll have proof."

"I'm listening."

"We're bringing you the crown of pearls."

Fish heard the real estate mogul make a noise as if a hook had lodged in his throat. "The sacred crown exists?"

"Seems more cursed than sacred. But yes, I have it. Along with the rest of the treasure. Call Barbie at sunset. Invite her over for a private viewing."

"She only comes out during the witching hour before dawn. When the air is cleanest. Free of certain particulates."

"I'm sure you can persuade her."

"What's in it for me?"

In the distance, Fish could see the outline of Tortuga Island, and beyond that the faint backdrop of mainland Mexico catching the evening's penultimate rays of sunlight. "First crack at the treasure."

"All of it?"

"I don't see why not."

"How much is there?"

"More than you can imagine. Tell Barbie to come alone."

"And when she arrives, where will this crown be?"

"Leave that to us."

"*Us?*"

"I'm bringing a friend."

Skegs gave a thumbs-up, beaming with pride.

Fish heard the rich man pause. "You and this friend—"

"Will be waiting on board."

CHAPTER FORTY-FIVE

Pacific Ocean, Baja California Sur

Toozie awoke trussed to a fighting chair on the deck of a yacht, the sound of diesel engines rumbling beneath her. Her head ached from the chloroform, her vision blurred. The mackerel sky ebbed sanguine in the fading light. A stiffening breeze had slapped her awake, and in the deepening shadows she could make out a rolling sea stretching into the distance.

"We're screwed," came a man's voice from beneath the stern gunwale.

Toozie gave a startled gasp. She glanced down and saw a dark shape huddled on the deck. A bald man hugging his knees to his chest.

"You were in the room with the mannequins."

The man straightened his legs, and Toozie saw that he, too, was bound. "Fucking freak show."

"But why?"

"Barbie's a sick woman. She stole my art and tried to blackmail me. When I refused to pay up, she had one of her apes put me in a glass chamber and burned off my hair. Stole my boats. I expect she'll have us tortured next."

Toozie yanked at the fishing line pinning her wrists to the armrests of the fighting chair.

"Forget it," the bald man said. "Eighty-pound test. Spectra. You'll never break it."

"Who's driving?"

"A real piece of shit. Calls himself Snake Hissken. Can you believe that crap? Has fangs and blood tattooed all over his arms."

"He knocked me out with chlorophyll."

"Gives me the creeps. Used to work for that other piece of shit, Ronald Stump."

Toozie stiffened.

"My thoughts exactly."

"Barbie and Stump are partners?"

"Apparently."

Toozie craned her neck and in the glow of the instrument panel could see the outline of the tall man.

"Is he alone?" she asked, turning back to the bald man.

"I think so."

"Do you know where he's taking us?"

"North. Around the arch and up toward Todos Santos."

"Todos Santos?" She felt her mind beginning to click, settling, freeing itself from the drug, working fast now. "At night? That doesn't make sense. There's no marina there. Nothing until—"

"Mag Bay."

She saw the bruise on the man's face and the blood around his nose. "You're hurt."

"Like I said, she's certifiable." He noticed her outfit. "You a cowgirl or something?"

"Something. It's nearly dark. Without the deck lights on, he can't see us."

"We're miles offshore. He knows we aren't going anywhere."

"Cut me loose."

He shook his head. "Suicide. Snake'll kill me for sure."

"You said he's going to torture you. How do you know he won't just kill you?"

"Barbie wants my money. She'll keep me alive as long as I agree to pay."

"And her partner, Stump?"

He shrugged, but she could see the worry in his eyes.

"Tell me your name."

"Charlie."

The veil of dusk finally ebbed, and in the boat's wake, Toozie could see stars begin to glimmer like ice chips. "Do you know why I'm here, Charlie?"

Charlie shrugged again.

"Bait."

"Bait?"

"I have something Barbie wants very badly."

"You print money?" he said sarcastically.

"Better than that. Baja's greatest treasure."

Charlie swallowed with difficulty. "Treasure?"

"*The* treasure, Charlie. From the time of the Jesuits. Gold, silver, pearls. Some say it's priceless."

"But…" he croaked.

"Barbie tried to steal it from my client."

"Slim Dixon is your client?"

Toozie struggled to contain her surprise. "You know Slim?"

"His brother offered to sell me the treasure. It was bullshit, of course. He works for Barbie, too. I'm beginning to think everybody does."

"I don't."

Charlie shrugged. "Not yet."

"Slim's dead."

Charlie stiffened.

"This isn't a game, Charlie. We're hostages. But I'm the one with the leverage. Cut me loose. It's our only chance."

"I have money," he protested. "Enough to buy my freedom."

"Small change compared to a sacred whale bone fitted with rare black pearls."

"The cursed crown," Charlie said reverently.

"Help me, Charlie, and I'll let you get first crack at it."

"What about Barbie and Stump? They have mountains of cash."

"The person in charge doesn't care about cash."

"He doesn't?"

Toozie shook her head.

"He won't sell to Barbie or Stump? No matter the offer?"

"Never."

Charlie's face broke into a grin.

"Now hurry and cut me loose before it's too late."

CHAPTER FORTY-SIX

Punta Baja, Baja California Sur

"The seaplane should have been back by now," Molly said, spackling a sheet of fiberglass over another bullet hole. She stood in the dinghy, her legs splayed from gunwale to gunwale, while Digby kneeled on the deck of the *Taliswoman* holding the dinghy tight to the hull with a bowline.

"Maybe there's trouble with the harbor master," Digby said. "A stolen fishing boat's a big deal."

Molly finished with the fiberglass and handed Digby the application tray. "Whatever the reason, it'll be dark soon."

Digby looked over at the cliffs stippled in shadow. When he turned back, Molly was climbing back aboard.

"You think Pancho's watching us?" he asked.

"Probably."

"Why hasn't he signaled us to come get the treasure?"

"I think we better go find out," she said and readied the dinghy.

"What about the twins? That guy Skegs said they were left tied up in the *mapache* cave."

Molly looked up at the cliff and the entrance to the cave. "If they were still there we'd have seen them by now."

"Unless he killed them."

"Another reason to get the treasure and get the hell out of here."

She rummaged through a deck bin and removed two head-lamps, and ten minutes later they beached the dinghy on the shore below the cave. Dusk had spread its cape across the dirt path, blending it into the hillside. They turned on their headlamps and started up the rocky path toward the *mapache* cave.

"I have a bad feeling about this," Digby said, tugging at his mustache. "I really hope they're not dead."

"If he shot them, we'd have heard the gunshots. Sound travels on water."

"He could have smashed their heads with rocks."

Molly shook her head. "It doesn't make sense to kill them *before* he had the treasure. Skegs said they were tied up in front of the cave. I think they were the cowboy's insurance. In case we didn't have the treasure."

"We don't."

"But he didn't know that when he left."

Digby slowed. "And now a man's dead. All because I stumbled across that old map."

She reached out and squeezed his arm. "It's not just some old map. And that man fired into my boat hoping to kill us. That was *his* choice, not yours."

"I dig around for old stuff. I find fossils. This morning I found a guy's ear. Jesus Christ, I spent all afternoon scrubbing a dead guy's blood from the floor of your boat."

"Because of a criminal. Not because of you. Your job is to uncover the past so that cultures can better understand history. This time you uncovered something rare and valuable. And that can bring out the worst in people. But finding that treasure is important for the people of Mexico. And I know how important it is to you." She took his hand in hers.

"Not anymore. Let's sail away from here and forget about all about it."

Molly looked over his shoulder and out at the bay where the *Taliswoman* was bathed in starlight. "Maybe we'd forget for a while. But then the regret would work its way in. I don't want you to live the rest of your life wondering what if. I don't want to live like that."

"But I don't care about the fame or the money anymore."

"I know you don't."

"Then what are we doing?"

"Making things right. For the indigenous people of Baja who were forced to work the mines. For all the people who died for that treasure." She released his hand and started back up the path shining her headlamp into the cave. "No dead bodies. The twins are gone."

"The hermit must have untied them," Digby said.

"I'd bet my boat on it," Molly agreed, racing up the cliffside as quick as a cat in the dark.

CHAPTER FORTY-SEVEN

Cabo San Lucas, Baja California Sur

Fish and Skegs splashed down on Cabo San Lucas Bay under a margarita sky. The cruise ships had departed, freeing the air of parasailers for the first time since dawn. The plethora of personal watercraft had been beached for the night, along with the floating trampolines, the barge bars, and the squadrons of glass-bottom boats. The shorefront cantinas had wrapped up their wet T-shirt contests, and the coastline of roped-off swimming areas had a brief respite from the schools of drunken tourists. Only an evening breeze ruffled the famous bay.

"Feels like old times," Skegs said munching on a stick of fish jerky. "Hey this is pretty good." He handed the bag to Fish.

"I've never seen it so calm."

"Well…" He pointed toward the marina, where a crush of sunset-cruise catamarans chugged from the entrance toward the rock arch, drunken revelers spilling over the double-stacked decks like locusts.

Fish swallowed a mouthful of jerky. "A little late. Sunset's almost over."

"Not in Cabo. They project one under the arch. Neon sunsets guaranteed to blow your mind."

"You're kidding."

"Just like Vegas, baby."

Fish landed far from the catamarans. "Still seems eerily quiet."

"Got to be a rave somewhere." Skegs dropped the seaplane's anchor out the cargo door. "Sammy's probably signing breasts at Cabo Wabo."

Both men laughed.

"We using the outboard?" Skegs asked as he deployed the dinghy.

"The sooner we get in and out the better," Fish said, and belted a sheathed machete to his pant leg.

"Not sure we should use the dinghy dock," Skegs said. "Marina's usually a nonstop fiesta. Guy like you might stand out. Like a bum in Beverly Hills."

"I'll take that as a compliment."

Skegs locked a four-horsepower Yamaha to the stern. "*Listo*?"

"Almost." Fish ignored the pain in his shoulder and unlatched a secret compartment beneath the passenger seat and handed Skegs a revolver.

"Now you're talking."

"Discretion's not your strong suit. Use only if necessary."

"Ah man, Indians can be discreet. How do you think we snuck up on all those white guys?" Skegs shoved the gun into the pocket of his windbreaker. The rest of his outfit was comprised of cutoffs, huaraches, and a backward-facing baseball cap. "But if that one-eyed Snake dude's around, all bets are off."

Fish shouldered the knapsack with the crown of pearls opposite his wound and boarded the dinghy. "Leave Hissken to me. And you're right about the dinghy dock. I'd rather we tie off directly to Stump's yacht."

"Hell yeah! Show the Rain King who's boss."

Fifteen minutes later they bellied up to the 200-foot mega-yacht rising like an acropolis in the nighttime. They quickly secured the bowline to a stern cleat, climbed the shiny stainless-steel ladder, and strode casually to the lower deck salon, where the familiar man in the gold-trimmed sailor's outfit stood guard.

"Howdy partner," Fish said and tipped his fish-skinned cap. "Stump's expecting us."

The man eyed the machete tied to Fish's thigh, and pulled a walkie-talkie from his belt. As he started to speak, Fish and Skegs pushed past him into the salon, closing the glass French doors behind them.

Fish unslung the knapsack from his shoulder and set it on a glass table with beveled edges trimmed in gold. Skegs waited by the door, pistol clutched tightly in his windbreaker pocket.

"We've got trouble, boss," he said as a hive of men appeared outside the glass doors. They parted and Ronald Stump stepped forward. He opened the doors, barely acknowledged Skegs, and entered the salon.

"A bit of decorum would be nice once in a while," he said to Fish.

Fish opened the knapsack and placed the crown to the center of the table. "I left Mephistopheles behind. That's all the decorum I could muster."

A short gasp escaped Stump's ever-present pout. His hangdog eyes popped with electricity, and his mouth parted into a corkscrew grin.

"My God," he muttered.

"Call Barbie," Fish said. "Tell her you don't give a shit about air quality. Tell her to be here in one hour. If not, this crown disappears forever. If she balks, tell her you had Slim followed. That he's dead. Along with that menacing American expatriate."

Stump's eyes never left the crown. "And the archaeologist?"

"Dead, too."

"I'm quite the killer."

"You only hire the best."

"Where's the rest of it?"

"In protective custody. Make the call. Describe the crown. Tell her it's for sale. But only if she comes alone."

Stump nodded.

"After the phone call, have one of your minions bring back my million." Fish tossed him the empty knapsack. "Where's Snake?"

"AWOL."

"He paid me a visit this morning. I sent him back with a message for you."

"He never showed up."

Fish gave the real estate mogul an inquisitive look.

"Barbie loaned him the car. Seems he's switched teams."

"Call her," Fish said, unsheathing his machete. "Now!"

CHAPTER FORTY-EIGHT

Pacific Ocean, Baja California Sur

Toozie may have lived in the desert, but she was at home on the water. An angler since childhood, she'd fished every lake and stream in Arizona. She owned a seventeen-foot Ranger bass boat and held the Arivaca Lake record for largemouth bass. And at least once a year, she traveled to the coast of California for yellow-fin tuna and albacore off San Diego. La Paz for dorado and wahoo, Buena Vista for yellowtail and roosterfish. And the innumerable trips to Cabo San Lucas, before the madness set in. Back when the billfish were plentiful and sharks spawned off land's end. Back when fifty-pound bull dorado were commonplace.

She'd caught many of the big bulls over the years. Beautiful turquoise brutes with block heads thrashing beside the Mexican sportfisher. The captain quickly ending the battle with a heavy short-handled stick. A fish bat. Solid hardwood. Pine hollowed out and filled with a cement core. One well-aimed strike capable of crushing bone and brain.

Brutal.

Effective.

Bloody.

Toozie thought of those big powerful dorado as she gripped the handle of Charlie Diamond's fish bat. Brazilian hardwood dipped in brass. Leather cord wrapped tightly around her wrist. Custom-made for wealthy big-game hunters. Heavier than any homemade Mexican fish bat.

And deadlier.

Toozie crept to the base of the helm ladder and glanced back at Charlie, who sat slumped in the fighting chair, hiding his baldness. In case Snake Hissken peered down on his hostage, manacled with fishing line to the fighting chair. A shiny pate reflecting starlight would give up the ruse. The dearth of deck lighting would help sell the switch. That and the kidnapper's impaired vision.

Satisfied, Toozie quietly climbed the helm ladder. The wheelhouse of the fifty-eight-foot *Queen of Diamonds* was expansive. Wall-to-wall electronics set into polished mahogany. A sloping, shatterproof windshield. Teakwood flooring and a hand-stitched leather captain's chair. A ceiling fan with wooden blades. Outside the helm, at the top of the stairs, was a landing with space for the captain to stand and watch the fishing lures skip across the wake. Space where Toozie now crouched, waiting for Charlie to call out.

To flush Snake from the helm.

In the confusion, Toozie would shatter the hit man's kneecaps. Buckle a shin. The tall man would fall. Maybe backward, maybe forward down the helm ladder. Either way, Toozie would be on him like a tomcat. The man didn't stand a chance.

Toozie stole a glance through the helm's rear window. Snake Hissken sat in the captain's chair smoking a cigarette, the back of his head silhouetted by the glowing instrument panel. She felt her heart race. She crouched, reached into her pocket for the fishing weight, and prepared to lob it to the back deck. Charlie's signal to wail.

Snake's voice inside the helm stopped her. She peeked through the window. The man was on a cell phone.

After a lengthy pause, she heard him say, "Hurry? You listen to me, Barbie. Tell that godless lawyer I've got his girlfriend. She may or may not be swimming with the sharks in a few minutes. As for Charlie, he'll definitely be swimming. I got no use for him."

Another pause. "Well, well, well, if it isn't the devil himself. Mr. Atticus Fish, aka Francis Finch, partnering up with that freak show, Barbie. Both of you can fuck off. I work for myself now."

Toozie watched Snake stand and pace the wheelhouse, his cigarette dangling from two long fingers.

"You want to see her again, you bring *me* the treasure!"

He blew a cloud of smoke toward the ceiling.

"You're lucky I don't kill her right now for you darting me with that voodoo shit this morning. But lucky for you, it cleared my mind. Lying at the bottom of that panga getting kicked by that fucking Indian brought me a vision. You giving Stump a million was too easy. Your donkey named Mephistopheles? That piece of shit cantina of yours named Heaven's Bar? You're a real comedian, Finch. I knew you looked familiar."

He paused to draw in another lungful of smoke. "Francis Finch the billionaire," he continued with an exhale. "Lawyer fucking Lucifer. I remember you. A lot of us wanted you dead. But you ran like a coward."

Another long pause and then, "So here's how it's going to work. I want *fifty* million in cash. *And* the treasure. I'll be at your bar tomorrow night. Bring me the money and the treasure. Then we'll take a little flight north in your plane. Drop me stateside, and when I'm safely across, you'll get your girlfriend back."

Toozie watched him snap the cell phone shut and toss it triumphantly to the dashboard. He ground his cigarette into the bubble compass and freed a pistol from his waistband. He turned. Toozie ducked.

Change of plan.

She rolled up her denim coat sleeves and cocked the fish bat with both hands, her heart pounding. She heard his footsteps. Muttering as he approached the helm door.

Incantations.

Biblical.

Bizarre.

He opened the door and stepped to the landing, his tall frame nearly invisible in the darkness. Toozie swung. She no longer aimed for the knees. Snake Hissken was a psychopath. A murderer planning to kill Charlie. A dangerous zealot. A deadly liability. She aimed high.

The bat cut through the air and slammed into Snake's lower lip, the heavy lumber steamrolling into his nostrils. Toozie followed through like a cleanup hitter and felt his nose flatten into his eye patch. The explosion of cartilage and blood was volcanic, the sound of shattering teeth and bone resonating above the rhythmic engine noise. Snake Hissken fell backward, his head bouncing hard off the edge of the mahogany dashboard.

Toozie leapt into the helm, hovering over her assailant, the fish bat raised high above her head. In case he moved. He didn't.

Snake Hissken's working eye had rolled up into his head, his mouth resembling a burst pomegranate. His eye patch dripped blood. Bits of skin and bone hung from his chin. Toozie watched his chest for movement.

Stillness.

The bat bounced across the floor, and Toozie bent forward, gripping her knees. Slowly she rose and staggered to the back landing. She reached out and gripped the railing for balance.

Then she fell to her knees and retched.

CHAPTER FORTY-NINE

Punta Baja, Baja California Sur

Halfway up the starlit slope, Molly heard a rock explode behind her. She stopped. A second rock ricocheted near her feet. She clicked off her headlamp and moved sideways in the dark.

"Pancho, it's me, Molly!" she called out.

"Go away," came a voice distinctly not Pancho's.

"Jack?"

The rock-thrower was silent.

"Where's Pancho?"

Another rock pinged in the distance.

"Jesus, Jack. Enough with the rocks."

"He told us to keep everyone away."

Molly slipped the backpack free of her shoulders and knelt to the rocks. She unzipped the top pocket and removed a loaded flare gun.

"Listen Jack," she said, moving invisibly among the rocks. "We're armed. You're not."

"We might be."

"If you were, you wouldn't be throwing rocks at my head."

"My brother don't have ears, but his eyes are working. You come any closer, he's gonna unload the big ones."

"We're not here to harm you, Jack."

"You could be working with that gunslinger. He left us down there to die."

"The cowboy's dead."

"How do we know you ain't lying?"

"Nobody's going to hurt you anymore, Jack."

Molly moved closer and ducked behind a large boulder. A rock exploded at her feet. She fired the flare. It rocketed through the night and erupted against the lava tubes in a shower of embers. Jack screamed.

Molly moved fast and moments later had Jack pinned to the ground.

"Don't kill me," he begged.

"Nobody's killing anybody," Digby said, appearing suddenly from the darkness. "Where's your brother?"

"Inside the big tube over there. The hermit guy gave him some herbs. For the pain. It knocked him out cold."

"And Pancho?" Molly asked, pressing her knee across his neck. "Where did he go?"

"No idea," Jack croaked. "He rescued us after the gunslinger drove off. Brought us up here. Gave us water and food."

Molly eased off.

Digby said, "And just disappeared?"

Jack rubbed the side of his neck. "He said he needed to move the treasure. Told us not to follow him. Said the lava tubes were dangerous. Filled with bats and snakes and shit." He shivered.

Molly dug inside her backpack and removed two pairs of boating gloves. She tossed a pair to Digby. Then she grabbed the guide rope and started down the main tube. Digby dropped in behind her.

"Hey, you can't go in there," Jack called out.

Digby pulled himself from the tube and pointed the flare gun. "That treasure's been stolen twice in as many days. I suggest you stay the hell out of our way."

CHAPTER FIFTY

Cabo San Lucas, Baja California Sur

Exactly one hour after Ronald Stump convinced Barbie to come to his yacht to view the infamous crown, the dance club owner crept into the salon of the mega-yacht like a mechanized wax figure. She wore a full snowsuit with its hood pulled tight, oversize wraparound sunglasses, starch-white gloves, and lace-up pink UGGs. Her nose and mouth were covered with a heavy-duty filter mask. The swaths of exposed skin at her temples and cheeks were heavily oiled with antibacterial cream.

"You better not be fucking with me," she snarled, her falsetto muffled behind the mask.

Stump peered out from the large screen. "Look at you. It's ninety degrees outside and you're bundled up like an Eskimo. The only person fucking with you is *you*."

Barbie swiveled her head around the room. Stump waited. Barbie gasped and raised a gloved hand to her filter mask.

She floated to the glass table. "Exquisite…" She reached out to touch the crown.

"And covered in ancient bugs. Polio, black plague, syphilis… gold fever."

Barbie jumped back. "Gold fever?"

"One of the worst. Destroyed some of the best and wealthiest merchants in the world."

She was giving him a perplexed look when the salon doors flung open and Fish entered the room. Barbie shrunk back in terror.

"I can't say that it's a pleasure to meet you," Fish said.

"Oh no," Barbie sputtered, backing away.

From the other side of the salon, the galley door opened and Skegs walked in.

"Oh my God!" Barbie cried out, and skittered into a corner.

"Easy now," Skegs said. "We've had our shots. At least I have."

Barbie blinked at the television screen. "Ronald?" she pleaded. "Why are these unclean men here?"

"Meet Mr. Atticus Fish and Mr. Skegs. Purveyors of the crown. It appears they hold all the cards at the moment."

Barbie dug a shaky hand into the pocket of her snowsuit and freed an electronic cigarette. "This wasn't our agreement, Mr. Fish."

"To be honest, I didn't care much for the terms." Fish took two lunging steps forward and gripped Barbie by the arm. "Release her immediately. Or we expose you to some very nasty microbes."

Barbie shrieked and dropped the cigarette. "Is that blood?" she asked, lifting her sunglasses just enough to gape at Fish's wounded shoulder.

"Now!"

Barbie fumbled with a different pocket and removed a cell phone covered in cellophane. She dialed.

Fish stepped in close. "Speaker phone."

Barbie shied away and pressed the button.

"Where is she?" Fish asked as the phone began to ring.

"On a boat."

After the third ring a man said, "Yeah."

"I need you to return immediately," Barbie said. "Bring back the woman. I'm being held hostage by her boyfriend. You must hurry."

"Hurry? You listen to me, Barbie. Tell that godless lawyer I've got his girlfriend. She may or may not be swimming with the sharks in a few minutes. As for Charlie, he'll definitely be swimming. I've got no use for him."

Barbie cleared her throat, birdlike, but Fish cut her off in midthought: "It seems you forgot to deliver my message to your boss."

"Well, well, well, if it isn't the devil himself. Mr. Atticus Fish, aka Francis Finch, partnering up with that freak show, Barbie. Both of you can fuck off. I work for myself now."

"Think, Snake. I have the treasure. I also have Barbie. Stump is with me as well. Bring me Toozie and it's all yours."

"You want to see her again, you bring *me* the treasure."

"Where?"

"You're lucky I don't kill her right now for you darting me with that voodoo shit this morning. But lucky for you, it cleared my mind. Lying at the bottom of that panga getting kicked by that fucking Indian brought me a vision. You giving Stump a million was too easy. Your donkey named Mephistopheles? That piece of shit cantina of yours named Heaven's Bar? You're a real comedian, Finch. I knew you looked familiar."

"I'm only going to ask one more time, Hissken. Where is she?"

Fish heard his nemesis exhale and then say, "Francis Finch the billionaire. Lawyer fucking Lucifer. I remember you. A lot of us wanted you dead. But you ran like a coward."

"You were quite the fanatic back then," Fish said. Jesus, even among the horde of enraged crazies who'd come after him, how could he have misplaced this lunatic and his Christ skull tattoo? "You had more hair back then. And both eyes. Still drinking the Kool-Aid, I see. Now where is she?"

"So here's how it's going to work. I want *fifty* million in cash. *And* the treasure. I'll be at your bar tomorrow night. Bring me the money and the treasure. Then we'll take a little flight north in your plane. Drop me stateside, and when I'm safely across, you'll get your girlfriend back."

The room filled with the ominous sound of a dial tone. Fish tossed the phone to Skegs, and moved so fast that Barbie could only gasp when he tore the filter mask from her face. "You've got three seconds to tell me where Snake is transporting her."

"Magdalena Bay," Barbie chirped before crumpling to the floor unconscious.

CHAPTER FIFTY-ONE

Pacific Ocean, Baja California Sur

After getting sick, Toozie reentered the helm. She throttled the engines back to neutral and then heard footsteps behind her. Charlie Diamond stepped to the doorway, gaping at Snake's body.

"Jesus, I thought the plan was to disable him."

"He was coming down to kill you."

Charlie's face paled.

"I overheard him on the phone. He demanded fifty million for my life. And the treasure."

"Son of a bitch," he said and kicked the dead man in the ribs.

Toozie turned back to the dashboard. "Can you engage the running lights for me?"

"The *what*?"

"Running lights. So we don't get run down by a shrimper or a freighter."

Charlie gave a weak shrug. "Sorry."

"I thought you said this was your boat."

"I hire a captain to take me fishing."

"You've never driven your own boat?"

"*Boats*," Charlie said, shaking his head. He bent down for a close look at Snake's face. "You did this with one swing?"

"Got 'em," she said, and flipped a stainless-steel toggle. A red glow appeared through the portside window. The starboard window reflected a greenish light.

"I can't believe he's dead."

"Believe it. Now grab all the rags you've got on board." Toozie retrieved the cell phone from the dashboard where Snake had tossed it. "And fill a bucket with soapy water."

"What about him?"

"Burial at sea," she said and dialed the phone.

Fish and Skegs transferred the unconscious Barbie along with the crown and the million in cash from Stump's mega-yacht to the seaplane, and then rounded the tip of the Baja peninsula and lifted off following the Pacific coastline north toward Magdalena Bay. It was nearing midnight and the moonless sky spread stars like icing across the sky.

"You think Snake's got his running lights on?" Skegs asked, as they flew past Todos Santos.

"Doubt it," Fish said. "He knows we'll be coming."

Skegs looked toward the back of the plane. "You think Miss Freak Show's going to wake up anytime soon?"

"Hope so."

"Should we tie her down?"

Fish craned his neck and observed Barbie, prostrate across one of Mephistopheles's hay bales, her eyes closed, the hood lowered from her bald head, the filter mask gone from her face.

"You worried she'll rush us?"

"She's crazy, man."

"She'll go limp with fright the minute she smells the essence of manure back there."

"Have a heart attack's more like it."

They stayed within five hundred feet of the water. Skegs pointed through the windshield at a blossom of phosphorescent water. Streaks of glow-stick green flashing in all directions like an underwater fireworks display.

"Dolphins feeding in the bioluminescence," Fish said.

"Or fucking."

Fish eyed his friend.

"I'm just saying we're not all that far from Cabo."

Fish was about to comment when a commotion at the rear of the plane caused them both to turn. Barbie was standing, her face a portrait of terror. She danced in a tight circle, shrieking.

"Whoa, now!" Skegs called out.

Barbie rose to her tiptoes, babbling incoherently.

Fish clicked on the interior lights. "You're okay. It's just us."

Barbie blinked rapidly, vacantly. Her muttering rose in volume, and then her eyes fell upon the cargo door. She raced toward it.

"Uh-oh," Skegs said, unbuckling.

He dived from his seat as a whooshing sound filled the cockpit. The door slid open and Barbie stared out into the darkness. Skegs grabbed an UGG lace-up boot.

Barbie leaped.

Skegs felt the boot release its foot. He crawled to the open cargo door and peered down as bits of straw swirled around his head and into the night sky. He dropped the boot into the void and slid the door shut.

"So much for killer germs," Skegs said, retaking his copilot seat.

"You almost saved her," Fish said. "There was nothing else you could do."

"I could have tied her up."

"Except we never—" Fish stopped and leaned across the plane's dashboard. "Running lights!" He pointed. "A mile or so ahead." He reached down to the console and raised a pair of binoculars. "Yacht. Dead in the water." He handed the glasses to Skegs when his cell phone buzzed.

"Yes?" he said, not recognizing the incoming number.

"Atticus, it's me, Toozie. We're on a boat. The man with the eye patch is dead."

CHAPTER FIFTY-TWO

Punta Baja, Baja California Sur

Pancho knew they'd come. He'd spent most of the night transferring the treasure through the maze of lava tubes. Hundreds of hollow passages snaking down the mountainside. Pancho knew them all. He knew the routes that coursed sideways, the ones that crisscrossed, doubled back, and dead-ended. The tubes that narrowed until a man had to belly crawl across shards of dried magma as sharp as cut glass. The ones that held bats, snakes, and raccoons. Most torqued and strangled into shale and bedrock. Others twisted to nowhere like a ball of tossed yarn. And a few opened onto the cactus-covered hillside hundreds of yards above the waterline.

But one managed its way to the bay below. A winding chute the size of a mine shaft whose lava had once meandered purposefully downward and plunged into the sea. A red-hot Slinky snaking down the ancient hillside. Centuries of hurricanes and tropical storms had widened its core and softened its edges. Countless rockslides had tumbled overhead, burying it deeper and deeper beneath the rubble. A secret passageway frequented by centipedes and scorpions.

And a bearded anchorite with millions in treasure.

Pancho had watched from the seaside opening of the lava tube as the archaeologist and his girlfriend returned near dark. Watched as they searched the *mapache* cave and then scaled the hillside in search of the twins. When the flare scorched his hideaway, he commandeered their abandoned dinghy. The couple would enter the tubes in search of the treasure. Of that he was sure. They'd follow his guide rope, expecting to surprise the keeper of the treasure. A guide rope that now led nowhere. It would take them hours to untangle themselves from the web of tunnels. Hours to backtrack or, if they were lucky, hours to descend to the sea cave. Either way, it gave him ample time to row the dinghy back and forth from the sea cave. Transport tackle box after tackle box of priceless loot to the sailboat.

Now, as Pancho pulled the paddles through the water one final time, he felt content. The bow of the inflatable bounced off the stern of the *Taliswoman*, and he scrambled aboard. He tied the bowline to a cleat and pulled anchor. He may have been a recluse, but he was no misanthrope. He'd had a trade once. Made a living wage working the shipyards at Pichilingue, just north of La Paz. Boats of all sizes. Rusted freighters, rotting ferries, yachts in need of bottom paint. And sailboats. Lots of sailboats. It may have been a decade since he'd been aboard a masted vessel, but sailing was like a long-term relationship.

Manageable when calm.

Pancho hoisted the mainsail and marveled at the way it caught the predawn breeze. He turned toward the east, smiling at the gentle rise of the schooner's bow. The pleasant rush of seawater across its hull. The sky was clear, and the sea mirrored dozens of familiar constellations. A pair of elegant terns chattered near astern and flittered off into the darkness.

Pancho squinted into the distance and saw the faint glow of Santa Rosalia and, beyond that, the abandoned rock quarry. He set the desired course. He'd anchor the sailboat off the scree-covered shore, and row the dinghy back to the old marina. Arrange for an old truck. Use one of the gold pesos. Drive back to the quarry and load the treasure. Leave the sailboat at anchor, and drive into the desert. Into the wastelands of the Vizcaino.

He was an old man now. A simple man with no need for riches. A man accustomed to hardship. His wife and children dead fifty years. The ferryboat accident a memory long buried by the clockworks of time. The downward spiral of a young man's life barely an afterthought anymore. He'd all but forgotten the corrupt investigation, and then the grieving husband's retribution. The nighttime firebombing of the ferry dock in La Paz.

The years in prison.

Pancho spent ten years in a cell not far from the old rock quarry. Years of tedium, of boredom, of books. History books, mostly. Exposing the oppression of his ancestors at the hands of foreigners. Jesuits, Franciscans, Dominicans. Priests who enslaved the locals and amassed a fortune. A fortune in treasure. A treasure never found. A treasure turned to legend.

Pancho left prison alone and penniless. He wandered the desert in search of history, of gold. But like so many before him, the hope proved futile, and Pancho settled in the lava caves above Punta Baja, spending his days drying fish and ferreting water and all but giving up on the treasure. Until two trucks rambled down the arroyo with a boat tied to the rack.

At first he thought they were tourists coming to fish one of Baja's most remote shorelines. He'd seen the occasional camper over the years. But the rocky beach was uninviting and most campers soon left.

These three, however, were different.

Unequivocally different.

One was bound by the wrists. Another carried a gun. Then came the stingray incident and the *mapache* attack. A sudden squall allowed Pancho to creep closer, and when the sky cleared he watched in wonderment as load after load of treasure was carried into the cave. The kidnapped man was suddenly in charge, and remarkably—impossibly—was leaving the treasure behind.

Treasure forged by the blood of Pancho's ancestors.

Treasure belonging to no one.

Treasure destined for reburial.

CHAPTER FIFTY-THREE

Punta Baja, Baja California Sur

By the time Digby and Molly emerged from the lava tubes it was daybreak. They were bruised from hours of ducking centuries-old magma, their knees bloody from tripping on unseen ridges of slag, their skin covered in basalt.

They splashed from the sea cave and swam to shore, Molly holding her backpack above her head.

Digby shivered in the dawn air, a smile breaching his blond mustache.

Molly loosened her light-coral ponytail and shook the water from her hair. She dropped the pack to the ground, rested her hands on her knees, and said, "Long night."

"Oh no."

Molly straightened.

"The dinghy's gone," Digby said.

Molly followed his eyes up the shoreline, and then glanced toward the glare of first light. She cursed, and then broke into a sprint.

"Where are you going?" Digby called out.

"He took the *Taliswoman!*"

Digby shaded his eyes from the rising sun and saw the empty bay. He grabbed the backpack and chased Molly up the path toward the *mapache* cave.

"He planned it all along," she panted ahead of him, scanning the horizon.

Digby lowered his eyes in disappointment.

"That speech about the blood of his people and the treasure belonging to no one. He played us, Digby."

"It's all my fault."

"Follow me," she said and started up the hillside.

"Where?"

"Higher ground. The *Taliswoman*'s mast is fifty feet tall. If I can spot it we can get an idea of where he's headed."

Digby followed and minutes later they stood at the entrance to Pancho's lava tubes.

"The twins are gone," she said.

"They were in on it all along?"

Molly didn't answer. She cupped her eyes and scanned the horizon.

"He's headed for Santa Rosalia."

"He is?" Digby asked excitedly.

"There." She pointed. "Just right of the sun. You can just make it out. That's her. No doubt about it."

Digby squinted. "I don't see it."

The sound of an engine brought their attention to the arroyo, where Digby's truck had suddenly come to life.

"The twins!" Digby screamed.

CHAPTER FIFTY-FOUR

Sea of Cortez, Baja California Sur

After scrubbing blood from the wheelhouse of the *Queen of Diamonds*, and weighing down Snake Hissken's body for a watery grave, Fish and Skegs gave Charlie Diamond a crash course in boatmanship. Toozie, who'd been down below rinsing blood spray from her blouse, joined them on the back deck as they prepared to leave.

"You sure you don't want me to look at those wounds?"

"They're fine."

"Gangrenous is more like it," Skegs said.

"I promise I'll see the doc when we get home." He limped across the back deck and opened the stern door. Turning to Charlie, he said, "Cabo's not safe for you. Stay on the compass heading we gave you and anchor in the shallows in front of Cantina del Cielo. We'll meet up with you later today."

"Barbie really offed herself?" Charlie asked.

Skegs shrugged. "More like an accident." He passed through the stern door and kneeled to the dive step where the dinghy was tied to a cleat.

Charlie said, "She stole my artwork, you know."

"Maybe now you'll get it back," Fish offered. "You should write down the heading I gave you. It's important."

"Can I see the treasure?"

"No."

"I saved your girlfriend."

"*Girlfriend* sounds so...'90s," Toozie interrupted. A breeze pushed a bang of burgundy hair across her face. She brushed it back and said, "I prefer *partner*."

Charlie shrugged. "A reward would be nice, then. Maybe a small piece of it. An ancient candelabra or something."

Fish gave him a look of astonishment. "Toozie hits a home run with Snake's face, and I'm supposed to give *you* a candelabra?"

Charlie was silent.

"Meet us at the cantina tonight. Dinner's on the house. We'll straighten everything out then."

Two hours later, as day broke over the Sea of Cortez, Fish opened his eyes. He disengaged the seaplane's autopilot and oriented himself. They were half an hour from Santa Rosalia, vectoring up the coastline. He lazily retrieved the binoculars from the dashboard and, seconds later, shook Skegs awake.

"Not now, honey," Skegs muttered and turned away.

Fish punched him in the arm.

"Ouch!" Skegs bolted upright, fists balled. "What was that for?"

Fish handed him the binoculars. "Looks like our archaeologist had a change of heart."

Skegs peered through the binoculars. "It's anchored off the old rock quarry. Nobody's on deck. The mainsail's flapping all over the place. I don't like the look of it."

Fish banked the plane sharply.

"What happened?" Toozie yawned from the parachute seat behind Skegs. She unbuckled and leaned into the cockpit and helped herself to the bag of fish jerky.

"Digby's anchored up just south of Santa Rosalia," Fish said. "Except they were supposed to wait for us at Punta Baja."

"Whoever smoked this fish knew what she was doing," Toozie said and accepted the binoculars from Skegs. "Why would they go ashore there?"

"Somebody must have met them with a vehicle. Taking the treasure north as fast as possible."

She handed the binoculars back to Skegs and took another slice of jerky. "You think the owner would just leave her sailboat behind?"

"Let's find out," Fish said, and ten minutes later taxied to the *Taliswoman* and shut off the engines.

"The dinghy's gone," Skegs said.

"You two have any weapons on board?" Toozie asked.

Fish glanced at Skegs.

"Ah, come on, man. You gave it to me."

"She's a professional."

"What, now I'm some amateur? She may have a license, but I'm the one with the warrior's blood."

"There's a filet knife in the back," Fish said.

Skegs reluctantly passed the handgun to Toozie. "You probably want me to launch the inflatable, too."

"Now that you mention it."

As dawn rolled its welcome mat to the horizon, they boarded the *Taliswoman*. Toozie ducked below deck, the pistol before her.

"All clear," she called out moments later.

"No signs of a struggle," Fish said, scanning the deck for blood or broken equipment.

Toozie poked her head out. "You might want to see this," she said.

They hurried down the ladder into the salon.

"On the table," she said, pointing toward the middle of the salon.

A silver bar the size of a tamale held down the corner of a note.

Fish shuffled to the table and freed the note. "It's in Spanish. From someone named Pancho."

"The hermit," Skegs said.

"Says he's grateful for the use of the boat, and that he's sorry. He hopes the silver bar will compensate for their troubles."

Skegs hefted the bar of silver and passed it between his hands. "Sorry, my ass. He's got all the loot. Never trust a hermit, man."

"He says he's reburying it in honor of his ancestors. Says the crown finally fulfilled its duty. Cursing all who tried to possess the treasure."

Skegs nearly dropped the bar. "What?" He snatched the note. "What a load of cow flap. No one *re*buries a zillion dollars worth of treasure."

Toozie chuckled. "Has a certain romance to it, I suppose."

"This isn't *Gone with the Wind*," Skegs commented, pocketing the silver. "What if it's all been a setup?"

"I don't follow," Fish said.

"Water leaves no tracks. Pancho took the dinghy. He could be headed to La Paz for all we know."

Toozie started up the ladder. "An old man in a cheap dinghy loaded with treasure might attract attention."

"What about the twins?" Skegs added. "They could be in on it, too."

Toozie stopped and glanced back at Fish.

"I forgot all about them," he said.

Thirty minutes later they landed at Punta Baja. Molly and Digby stood at the shoreline looking forlorn.

"Man are we glad to see you," Digby said when Fish stepped ashore. "Pancho stole Molly's boat."

"We know," Fish said.

"You found it?" Molly blurted.

"Anchored just south of Santa Rosalia."

"Anchored and abandoned," Skegs emphasized as he slid the dinghy up the rocks.

"And the treasure?" Digby asked.

"Gone," Skegs said, looking around. "Where'd the twins go?"

"Stole my truck."

"Man, I thought *I* was having a rough couple of days."

Toozie said, "Pancho left you a note. Said he's reburying the treasure."

"I don't want it anymore," Digby said.

"What the hell's wrong with everyone?" Skegs asked. "Some dirt-poor dude living in the rocks scribbles a few lines and we're just supposed to believe him?"

Toozie turned to Digby. "Want us to find him?"

"Not really."

Skegs choked out a laugh. "What he means is, hell yes, he wants you to find the old man who stole our treasure."

"*Our* treasure?" Fish asked.

"Let him be," Digby said. "I'm done with the archaeological business all together." He wrapped an arm around Molly's shoulders and kissed her on the cheek. "Sailing seems to suit me." He turned back to Toozie. "How much do I owe you?"

"Well—"

"I'm sure the silver bar will cover it," Fish interrupted, looking at Skegs.

They all turned.

Skegs reached into his pocket and handed the bar to Molly. "He left it on your boat. Along with an apology."

Molly handed it to Toozie. "Thank you." She looked at Fish and then to Skegs. "All of you."

"We still have the crown," Fish said.

Digby held up a palm. "I've had enough of curses."

"Shit," Skegs said. "Cursed ain't nothing but a state of mind."

"You saved our lives. Keep it."

Skegs nodded briskly. "Now you're talking."

Fish shook his head. "Retirement can be costly. I'll put it up for bid. Stump and Diamond will fight like weasels over it."

"The Mexican government might have something to say about that," Toozie said.

Digby agreed. "Too many questions about where it came from and where the rest of it is. Bureaucrats'll never believe our story about Pancho. I'd prefer to fly under the radar. Forever."

Fish shifted his weight to his good leg and said, "A sentiment I share. A bit tougher than it seems, however. I'll keep the auction selective and quite secret." Fish reached out and shook Digby's and Molly's hands in turn. "Stop by my cantina next time you're in Mag Bay. Pick up the money for the crown."

"Minus the auctioneer's fee," Skegs chimed in.

"Ten percent sound fair?" Digby offered.

Skegs's mouth unhinged.

Fish turned to Toozie. "Ever been in a submarine?"

"I can't say that I have."

"Landed a black snook?"

"Nope."

"Scratch the belly of a drunken iguana?"

"Definitely not."

"Got any plans for the next few weeks?"

Toozie slipped her hand inside of his, her opal eyes dancing with the incoming tide. "I do now."

THE END

Jack and Zack pulled into the gas station outside Santa Rosalia and parked Digby's truck beneath the awning.

"Fill 'er up," Jack said to the attendant. They had no money, so he kept the engine running for a fast getaway.

"You look familiar," the man said in broken English.

"Huh?"

"You and your brother are *muy famosos*."

"Oh yeah?"

He pointed at Zack. "*El mapache grande*."

The skin beneath Jack's working eye wrinkled into a vise.

"And you, amigo." He pointed at Jack's eye. "*Que raya tan grande*."

"Yeah, big fucking *raya*. Whatever the hell that is. We're in a hurry, okay?"

The man smiled, but his eyes held no mirth. "*Donde está el vaquero?*"

"The *what*?"

"Cowboy. The hombre with the gun."

"I don't know what you're talking about." Jack tried to engage the gears, but the man deftly reached in, shut off the motor, and snatched the keys.

"What the fuck?"

"My brother's the dockmaster."

"Give me back the keys."

"He drove you to the hospital. His wife works the emergency room."

"Do I look like I give a shit?" Jack said, glancing nervously to Zack, whose ears couldn't hear the conversation, but whose eyes had widened with concern.

"You didn't pay your hospital bill."

"Jesus Christ. That's what this is all about? We were kidnapped and tortured by that fucking cowboy. He took all our money." He reached out the window for the keys. "My brother needs to get home. To get his ears fixed."

The gas station attendant pocketed the keys. "We have doctors here."

"We need a specialist."

"First you pay the bill."

"This is bullshit," Jack said, opening the door.

The man lifted his shirt, exposing the butt of a pistol.

Jack closed the door.

"Maybe we make a deal."

"What kind of deal?"

"Give me the truck, and I pay your bill."

"How much is the bill?"

"*Mucho.*"

"How the hell we gonna get home without a truck?"

The man's smile was inviting this time. "My other brother, he works at the bus station."

Charlie Diamond sat at the helm of the *Queen of Diamonds* drinking his fifth Cape Cod of the morning. He'd started with one of the cranberry cocktails to celebrate Barbie's passing. Then another when the sun rose. A third, as he found the shoreline and angled close.

"To hell with a compass heading," he said aloud and poured himself a fourth Cape Cod.

He spent the next thirty minutes following the coastline and celebrating his entrance into Magdalena Bay a hero. He planned to anchor off the expatriate's bar, swim in like an Olympic athlete, and demand a round of well-deserved mango margaritas for the waiting crowd.

But then a morning fog bank rolled in and blanketed the shoreline. It swallowed Charlie and his boat, growing thicker by the minute. Charlie began to sweat. He immediately poured a hefty fifth cocktail and summarily forgot the compass heading.

Now, as he finished the double-strength drink, he squinted through the mist and shrieked. An enormous rock loomed up like a behemoth in front of the bow. Charlie spun the wheel and heard the stainless-steel bowsprit crumple like foil. The fiberglass prow splintered, and Charlie fell across the dashboard, losing his vodka cranberry. The sound of shattering glass was quickly muffled by the snapping of bulkhead support beams. Charlie abandoned the steering wheel and frantically flipped every switch on the dashboard.

The unmanned steering wheel was spinning the boat in a tight circle when a sudden clattering of heavy metal filled the air. The anchor had released, and thirty feet of chain dropped to the ocean floor. Charlie immediately reversed the switches. The anchor wench reengaged. The anchor, however, had caught rock. The electric motor whined and the boat began to arch wildly. The chain groaned with tension and then cut through the broken bow like a fin through a wave. Charlie cringed. The boat slammed sideways into the same towering rock, shearing off most of the stern.

Charlie lunged for the throttle controls and yanked. The twin engines shuddered and reversed. The anchor broke free and the boat backed full speed into the boulder. The propellers churned to pieces and both drive shafts snapped. The engines died and seawater flooded the bilge.

Charlie grabbed the VHF radio and screamed Mayday until he was out of breath. He raced from the helm, grabbed the seat cushion from the fighting chair, and leapt overboard. The current pulled him away from the rock and out to sea.

Three hours later, his shaved head pulsing like a burning coal, Charlie heard the rumbling of an engine. He blinked through bloodshot eyes and spotted a mega-yacht bearing down on him. The boat slowed and the captain tossed a life ring.

"You're one lucky son of a bitch," Stump said, as Charlie crawled through the opened stern door. "My captain heard a distress call as we left Cabo. Here we are minding our own business, heading to Mag Bay, when you start screaming Mayday. He locked in on the coordinates. The fog lifted and a few hours later, he spots a reflection. Seems your new hairstyle saved your life."

"Mag Bay?" Charlie spluttered.

"Seems the expatriate has a crown he'd like to sell."

EPILOGUE THREE

Pancho couldn't believe his luck. After sailing Molly's schooner to the abandoned quarry south of Santa Rosalia, he'd off-loaded the treasure one tackle box at a time. He hid the loot in the rocks, and then anchored the sailboat with a note and a bar of silver. He deployed the dinghy and entered the old Santa Rosalia marina.

He needed something to transport the treasure inland. A rusted Volkswagen or old Toyota truck. Something large enough to hide his secret. An affordable junker he could purchase with the solid gold peso in his pocket.

As he walked the docks, an old man with a bird's-nest beard and no teeth emerged from a wrecked yawl. The man seemed drunk and soon had Pancho in conversation. Something about a stolen boat found floating off Punta Baja, and an abandoned convertible Cadillac parked just up the way. Pancho asked who owned the car. At first the old man just shrugged. Then Pancho displayed the gold peso.

An hour later, he sat behind the wheel of Slim's Caddy, heading south. He took the old quarry road, reloaded the treasure into the trunk, and by late afternoon was nearing the turnoff for the Santa Clara Mountains, deep in the middle of the Vizcaino desert.

All afternoon, he drove Slim's convertible Cadillac across the desert. The dirt road was rutted and dotted with desert sage, brittlebush, and lomboy, but the low-clearance car persevered without breaking an axle or blowing a tire. But for the occasional vapid-eyed cow or bleary-eyed buzzard perched atop a *cardón*, the terrain was deserted. It seemed humanity had abandoned the Vizcaino badlands. *And for good reason*, Pancho thought as he slowed for a sidewinder crossing the road. The relentless heat waffled the horizon and charred the desert, and without water and transportation a man would be lucky to survive a day.

Fortunately, Pancho had both.

The dirt road meandered toward a mesa, where it dropped into an expanse of cirio cacti with carrotlike tops covered in ball moss. The occasional elephant tree added to sparse landscape, and then the road suddenly deteriorated into barely recognizable ruts.

Pancho parked.

The late afternoon sun hovered at the horizon like a cobra. The hermit welcomed it. Only a fool would trespass the Vizcaino in summer. A fool or an old hermit with a trunk-load of treasure in need of a proper burial.

Pancho opened the Cadillac's trunk. Mounds of gold and silver winked in the sunshine. He filled the first tackle box and began walking. Thirty minutes later, he kneeled near a *tinajas* where a spring had once attracted indigenous tribes. Their ancient adobe walls had melted long ago, and all that remained of Baja's heartiest people was a barely discernible *hornito*.

Pancho began to dig. The top layer of crust soon unearthed bits of ancient ore. Two feet down, he hit the bones of an ancestor. He widened the hole, and then emptied the tackle box. The sun had finally set, and the jaundiced sky flared in celebration.

Pancho smiled. He looked up and thought of the men and women who long ago had survived the inhospitable Vizcaino.

His eyes misted as he gave thanks for their sacrifices.

Then he headed back to the Cadillac for another load.

I've often wondered what one would do upon finding the Jesuit Treasure. Alert the Mexican government? Secret the cache across the border in the back of a camper van? Twice in the last decade, I've found myself in a similar dilemma, both times after coming across kilos of marijuana floating in the Sea of Cortez. Pounds of pot free for the taking. Which became the impetus for *Wahoo Rhapsody*'s deckhand stuffing bricks of *mota* inside the bellies of dead tuna. But a chest full of Jesuit loot? Hmmm. I think we're going to need a bigger fish.

Speaking of fish, in September 2008, two commercial long-liners were nabbed just outside Magdalena Bay with twelve tons of illegally caught dorado on board. They'd netted the fish under the authority of sharking permits. The dorado were considered "bycatch," even though it was clear the long-liners were specifically targeting these vast schools of tasty game fish, and not the occasional mako or blue shark that cruised these waters. Twelve tons of dorado is a tremendous take, especially from an area so pristine that most visitors think it a protected sanctuary. I grew angry as I read the article in the *LA Times* ("Baja Bust Nets 10–12 Tons of Dorado"). I also knew that a man like Atticus Fish would take it upon himself to do something to stop it. Which was the impetus for the personal submarine with titanium blades.

And while this may be a book of fiction, many of the locations are real. Hussong's Cantina in Ensenada is one of the few bars that remains unchanged over the decades. Sawdust still covers the floor, and on any given night you'll squeeze by more locals in cowboy hats than tourists in straw ones. Mama Espinoza's Restaurant in El Rosario is another spot largely unchanged. If you head down that way, stop in for a lobster burrito. You'll be glad you did.

Punta Baja exists, as does the giant Baja California raccoon, known as *mapache grande*. In all of my years traveling south of the border I've only seen one of these strange creatures. It was at four in the morning while camping on a faraway Baja beach. The raccoon had wandered to the water's edge to forage on crabs and dead fish. When I illuminated it with a flashlight, I'm not sure who was more startled. A hiss and a growl was all it took to send me back inside my tent.

The sportfisher named *Con Limón* that Slim steals from the marina in Santa Rosalia is a fishable boat. It now sits in dry storage on the mainland side of the Sea of Cortez. But the owner has plans to move it back to Baja. Just as soon as I find the time. And, yes, Santa Rosalia has a terrific French bakery.

And what can I say about Cabo San Lucas that hasn't already been said in two novels? I'm saddened that it is no longer the dusty seaside village of yore, and even more saddened by the state of its offshore fishing. This one-of-a-kind locale has been overrun by commercial fishermen as well as tourists. As for my depictions of the chaos, rest assured the embellishments are minor. And if you have young children, spring break in Cabo is not recommended.

Before we leave the subject of Cabo, it should come as no surprise that the topless club in this book truly is located adjacent to a *farmacia* that displays enormous advertisements for erectile dysfunction drugs. It is a very popular *farmacia*. The club is located in Plaza del Sol. It's not called the Pink Octopus.

Slim's Elbow Room most definitely exists, but it was so crowded I couldn't get mine in. I did see iguanas across the street dressed up in silly garb. No one, to my knowledge, projects sunsets on Cabo's famous Land's End arch. I expect it to happen soon.

Pancho is based on a real character. The last time I saw him he was living alone on a beach far south of Bahía de los Ángeles. He wandered into our camp one night and told stories and danced and ate a live scorpion that had crawled onto a rock to escape our campfire.

And lastly, do I believe in the Jesuit Treasure? You bet. Have I found it? Probably not…

ACKNOWLEDGMENTS

Once again I am indebted to the kindness of Baja's residents, both local and expatriate. Their ingenuity under harsh conditions never ceases to amaze me.

A tip of the hat to the treasure hunters of yore like Nellie Cashman, Walter Henderson, J. W. Black Jr., Erle Stanley Gardner, and the writer Choral Pepper, who accompanied Gardner on many expeditions south of the border. She preserved her experience in a little book titled *Baja California: Vanished Missions, Lost Treasures, Strange Stories Tall and True.* And to Herman Hill, who may or may not have found a bit of the treasure over decades of scouring Baja's inhospitable deserts.

To John Minch and Thomas Leslie, who together (with illustrator Edwin Minch) compiled an exhaustive geological field guide of Baja titled *The Baja Highway.* To Tom and Shirley Miller and Carol Hoffman and Ginger Potter, whose detailed satellite space maps of Baja California have guided me across its back roads for decades. Known simply as *The Baja Book,* it is indispensable for Baja travelers in search of solitude.

To my compadres and early readers: Captain Winston Warr III, Douglas McFetters, Mickey Morey, Derek Crossley, and Randy Denis, who also moonlights as my cartographer. Your friendships are precious, your insights priceless.

To Claudia Solórzano for fixing my bad Spanish, and to my good pal Dr. Kent Nasser, whose intimate knowledge of portable manual external defibrillators helped Slim Dixon shock the twins into submission.

To Tyler Dilts, author of *A King of Infinite Space* and *The Pain Scale,* who got me started on this novel path. I loved your writing class so much I took it twice. An ocean of thanks, professor.

To Richard Pine and Inkwell Management. Your masterful direction with *Wahoo Rhapsody* led us to this point. Manuscripts become magic in your hands. I am forever grateful for your advice and kindness and belief in this series. If literary agency were an Olympic sport you'd hold the record for gold medals. Thank you, amigo!

A special shout-out to senior editor Andrew Bartlett, and his amazing team at Thomas & Mercer. Thank you for the opportunity to take Atticus, Skegs, and Toozie on to greater adventures and mayhem. They, and I, are forever indebted.

To David Downing, whose editing skills were a welcome sea breeze, and to Brian Bendlin and Phoebe Hwang, whose copy edits put the final shine on these pages.

To Jacque Ben-Zekry and her tireless marketing team. A book is only as good as its readership. Fathoms of gratitude for getting the word out.

And Baja hugs to my muse, Amanda Trefethen. Once again, you made my writing better, my plotting stronger, and my characters more believable. Not to mention my life more meaningful. The dream came true, thanks to you.

ABOUT THE AUTHOR

 Shaun Morey is the best-selling author of the *Incredible Fishing Stories* series and *Wahoo Rhapsody* and a contributor to magazines and newspapers worldwide. He won the inaugural Abbey-Hill short-story contest and is a three-time winner of the *Los Angeles Times* novel-writing contest. Over the years, he has worked as a bartender, a fishmonger, a surf instructor, and an attorney, while secretly planning his own escape into the badlands of Baja California.